My Words Were All I Had

My Words Were All I Had

WILLIAM SANCHEZ

ARPress
45 Dan Road Suite 5
Canton MA 02021

Hotline: 1(888) 821-0229
Fax: 1(508) 545-7580

Ordering Information:

Quantity sales. Special discounts are available on quantity purchases by corporations, associations, and others. For details, contact the publisher at the address above.

Printed in the United States of America.

ISBN-13:   Paperback   979-8-89356-055-8
                eBook   979-8-89356-056-5

Library of Congress Control Number: 2024903497

Table of Contents

Table of Contents

CHAPTER 1

The Coffee Shop

You're not just playing games, when you're playing with lives.

"Help me to understand, Sebastian. What is it that drives a man? To take the risk of approaching a woman, without a grain of thought on how to open up to her? Why would you walk over without not knowing what to say?" asked Mike.

As we were both admiring a pair of gorgeous ladies, who sat a few tables away from us. Seeming to be enjoying their own private conversation, just as much as we were discussing ours.

"I just can't get over the habit of having the moment lead the way for me," I explained. As I smirked at Mike's attentive stare, I started to school him. "Just calling a woman beautiful is not going to lead you that far, in some cases nowhere at all. But to make a woman feel beautiful, now you're entering a whole other world," I detailed.

He swiped the coffee off his mouth with a napkin faster than a credit card on the card reader. Then threw his hands up surrendering to my claims. "Okay then, you plan on performing hypnosis? Are they going to be in a trance by the time you introduce me?" he ques-tioned sarcastically.

"Nah man, I'm not doing nothing outrageous just yet," I reacted. I then waved my finger at him as I continued. "But… Whatever I do say, I'm going to make sure they both tell you. They've never been approached in such a manner," I predicted to Mike.

He remained in a daze trying to figure out my attempt. As he looked right at them, he informed me. "They've been staring at us for a while now, Sebastian."

"That's good!" I assured him. "That's what they are doing at the moment, if you pick actions of the moment, Mike. Then how can you ever sound rehearsed?" I asked.

He crossed his arms with a crumbling face of confusion. "So you're going to ask them what are they staring at?" he asked.

"No," I calmly answered.

There was a flier of an event on the table next to us. I had to think quick, as these two attractive ladies—one blonde and a bru-nette—at four tables away from us. Possibly interested, from what Mike and I had observed. Even though they were smiling at each other while sharing words, they would take glances in our direction. Our interest grew more as we noticed that the glancing became more frequent. Now maybe I could just approach and introduce myself, but I promised Mike I'd be different.

"Give me a pen!" I demanded.

"What? Are you drawing her something?" he joke.

"Shut up with that. And I'm glad you're wearing that leather jacket. It makes you look like a detective," I added. I then turned away from him.

"This is top of the line right here! You don't know about this!" Mike yelled as I walked off.

I then grabbed the flier on the next table faster than the girls could notice. As I approached the table, they leaned away looking up at me. Waiting to see what I had to say.

"I don't mean to interrupt your chatter over coffee, but I need to know. Which one of you is hired for the hit? And what's the motive?" I asked. As I had moved the pen and flier around, pretending to write a police report.

"Excuse me?" sked the blonde, confused, as if wanting me to repeat myself.

"Well, my friend Mike over there is very nervous. And he believes you girls have been staring because you're planning a killing of some sort. So what's the truth here?" I joked.

The brunette put a hand over her mouth, holding back her giggles in reaction when the blonde questioned me.

"Now why would you say that? We just like what we see, that's all".

"Thank you, and…this is just my way of saying hi," I confessed.

"Hmm…that's different," judged the blonde as I could feel I was being eye-scanned by her friend.

"I like a man who can be different," interrupted the brunette. With the help of such a comment, I already knew who I was to aim for.

"And your name is?" asked the brunette.

But even to say my name, I wanted to continue keeping this interaction interesting. "Since women love for men to guess their age, let's just say"—I paused briefly—"you two guess my name, and I'll do the same in return. And if you get mine right, then I won't arrest you two," I joked.

They laughed and accepted the challenge. "You look like a Carlos," said the brunette, while she looked me up and down. I pre-tended to be shocked to add a bit of fun.

"Me! Why, because I look Spanish?" I blurted. They both shook their heads no as I attempted take a small shot at assuming their names too. "Your friend here looks like a Bridget," I teased the brunette.

"What is a Bridget supposed to look like anyways?" she asked sarcastically.

I turned around to see if Mike was still sitting. He was smiling in our direction. The same way a child does when he sees his favorite playground from a car window as mommy drives by. I waved him down to come over, since we were pretty much done with our table.

"Would you ladies mind if we sit here with you two?"

"No, not at all," offered the blonde.

I placed my hand on Mike's shoulder as soon as he slid right next to me. "Hey, this is Mike by the way, and I'm Sebastian. Excuse the thirty-second delay of my name," I said.

"Well, I'm Anna," the blonde introduced herself.

"And I'm Lisa." That was the brunette.

This sweet-looking woman was the cream to a cake, but you wouldn't find a sweetie pie like her in any pastry shop. A grown woman's face with the eyes and smiles of a baby. Her body had more curves than a bowling pin. I was eager to have words with her. "So, Lisa, I must say that the whole glasses look goes perfect with you, it's cute," I complimented. I then calmly sat next to her.

"Oh! Well, thank you. And I only wear them because I need to. But I don't like wearing my glasses," she confessed. I leaned in toward her, getting my mouth close to her ear.

"If I needed glasses, using them would depend. For instance, as long as you're the one who comes into focus, I don't need glasses. Everything else can stay blurry," I flirted.

"Aww, thank you." She sighed. Blushing while she played with the back of her ear.

Now this was the type of interactions and exchange I was used to. But it was a role that was becoming old; it really wasn't my type of play anymore. I was soon to hit a wall of realization not long after us four had conversed for a bit.

"So, ladies!" shouted Mike, in an attempt to steal the show, as he had a suggestion to make. "Sebastian and I can take you two on a double date. Especially since Sebastian don't even look out his bedroom window, as of recently," he said. I rolled my eyes at him, and before he continued, he whispered to me: "Bro, I got you."

I noticed when I pulled my phone out. Lisa started to look around the ground almost like she'd lost something. I continued with my original intentions and asked for her number. I found it to be odd that she looked at me with wide eyes and turned to Anna to ask, "Can I give him yours?"

"Of course, girl, here's the phone. He can type it in," suggested Anna.

I was then curious to know. "So you don't have a phone?" She bit down on her lips for a second before she decides to explain. "It's that I'm married, but don't worry, he's never up my ass wondering where I'm at all times," she confessed. I sat there frozen, letting her continue. "Plus, I'm always with my best friend. So you can call me at her number whenever," she assured me.

I wasn't pleased with Mike being happy to hear this. And he reacted with excitement. "My man Sebastian!" said Mike. With his arm around Ana. He was enjoying himself as much as he was enjoy-ing my situation with Lisa.

To make better sense of this, I questioned her with an assump-tion. "I take it that you're heading for divorce or something?" I asked, as I looked at her hand trying to see a ring.

"No…he treats me pretty good" she addressed, before Ana then interrupted.

"He's actually a really nice guy, I get along with him well," she confessed.

This whole time, Mike was laughing and pushing my shoulder softly with his fist. While at this point I'm sitting with them, I pondered, what the hell am I doing? Not only was I seducing another man's wife, but these two girls were also admitting that he was a nice guy. They went as far as explaining features of the nice house he shared with Lisa and the great job that he had landed. I Felt a small wave of nausea settling in me. I then pulled Mike by his jacket and leaned him toward me to remind him. "Hey, don't we have a whole kitchen to rebuild?" I said. Then stared sharp in his eyes to signal that we were done here.

"Man, that's not until five o'clock. It's only 1:00 p.m. right now!" he reacted, annoyed.

"Yeah, sure, Mike, we got to go and pick up some stuff. Plus the machines," I demanded. I started getting up when Ana seeming to be bothered with my behavior.

Asked Mike, "Is everything okay?"

"Yes, yes!" I interrupted.

She leaned back and rolled her whole face at me; rude was what I seemed. But to close off this gathering in that fashion was the least of my worries. I still said bye even if it wasn't accepted with care. "We have to go, and it was nice to meet you two," I blurted. I then smacked Mike lightly on his back and whispered away from the girls, "If you want to get their numbers that's fine, but let's just go. I'll be in the truck."

He looked down and shook his head. I can tell he was aware I wasn't pleased with this encounter. But he knew there was more to my mood change than just the infidelity of Lisa. I then walked out of the coffee shop with a rhythm to my steps as if I had better things to do. We don't shed our old skin to then hang it up in the closet, just to wear it at a later time in life. We shed our old skin to make the space for a new skin to live our life in, until we keep growing. There is no emptier feeling than the feeling we get from the actions that don't define us anymore.

Even more when we recognize that these old actions have cost us the loss of so much. And walking away was the best action I took in this particular time.

Chapter 2

A Talk of Purpose with Mike

For losing his queen, life helps enroll a king into the school of many lessons.

Having plenty of work remodeling houses was a fact, me wanting to leave sooner than expected. Had all to do with how uncomfortable Lisa made me feel with her situation at home. While I was now sit-ting in the pick-up truck, I might as well have gone through the list of supplies Mike and I had to pick up for our project today. Before I could get to the bottom of the list, the driver door swung open, and Mike was shoving his head in the truck, not looking so friendly.

"What the hell just happened with you! I mean what now? We we're having a good time," aggravated, he exploded.

I exhaled slowly and took my time to have him learn something. "A good time, huh? These little adventures are not what I call a good time anymore. That woman had no reason, no excuse! To do what she was about to do with me," I argued. "What if I was her husband? What if?" His eyes were narrow the whole time. As if he understood another reason for my outburst. "I know you think it's funny play-ing these games and all. But sometimes, Mike, when we think we're playing games, we're actually playing with lives. And sometimes, we might just be playing ourselves the whole time," I finished saying. I felt a relief. My chest was as calm as still air after I spilled all this out. Mike sat down yapping with his hand like a puppet, giving me the sign that I'm just talking gibberish.

"Who you think you talking to, man? I used to be your wing-man at times. Should we reintroduce ourselves all over again? Because this is not you, bro," he described. He didn't speak another word after that, and started to drive off.

I had no plans on apologizing, but I did feel I had to explain myself. "I don't regret anything I've done. And I'm not saying I won't date around while I'm here single. I just don't feel the drive to be fast and crazy like we were ten years ago, bro!" I argued. He looked over at me and smirked. "What?" I yelled. "Go ahead…say it! What's that look for?"

His demeanor went as calm as someone who had just woken up in the morning. "I know what's wrong with you," he claimed.

I was confused as to where he was going with this. "What do you mean? I questioned. "What's wrong with me according to you?" I asked as I shook my head with sarcasm. I was upset at this point.

He suddenly started to speed through traffic. "Matter of fact, let me just show you the problem," he said, determined. Then he put the radio on and pretended that I wasn't even there.

After five minutes, I started noticing a particular route; these houses and streets seemed familiar. It made me anxious and both-ered. Since I'm one who hates surprises. And with my flesh sizzling from my boiling blood, I was not in the mood for such a thing. I slapped the volume button of the radio to mute the station. "All right! That's it, where you going with this?" I demanded of him to answer. He took one more turn, and there we were, behind the street that I once lived in, when I lived with Isabel. The only relationship I'd always regret. It was a very long street, but once we got to the actual house, he parked.

"We accidentally drove by this old place of yours a few weeks ago. I didn't want to say anything to you because I thought you were over her," he continued. "You can't be in love. I saw you happy it was over! But what I did notice, your whole mood as well as your thinking that day all changed after staring at that house, bro," he described. He took a pause for a moment to observe my reaction. I sat still, not saying a word. "You're like family to me. I just want to know if you are okay," said Mike.

And he was right, I had forgotten about Isabel. Or at least I thought I did. What I really did was block her out of my mind when I realized that I might have made a mistake leaving her. I refused to give myself the time to regret, the time to forgive myself, and most of all, the time to hurt and heal. I had gone on with my life dating women and having what I thought was some fun. Not expecting that this guilt was going to hit me at some point in the future. No matter how far I ran away from the feeling, I had to face it head on eventually.

"Listen, Mike…every step forward leaves a footprint on the ground that must stay behind. I cannot go back. I can accept that and that's fine!" I debated.

"So what is it?" he wondered.

I fixed myself in my seat, posing for comfort, and I started to go into detail on what I was feeling. "We had a fulfilling future to look forward to. I cut our growth in half by doing wrong by her side then leaving her, and now there's someone else growing with her. A healthy family and I respect that," I continued, recalling our past. "But when I last reflect on our past relationship, what bothers me is that I knew how and what parts that I could have fixed. But my ignorance at the time would not allow me to do the improvement. I wasn't even romantic with her like I was with random girls," I said.

He started to wave his arms around while he quoted something I've said before. "You know the human body's arms move many unique ways and all. But the arms on a clock only move in one direc-tion… forward. I heard you say that once, Sebastian."

"I know, I remember. I'm not saying I miss her. I'm just saying I learned so much from losing her," I confessed.

I fix homes for a living, but how was I living with myself now after knowing I took my own home apart? As I looked over at the house, I could still hear the echo of the exact words Isabel said to me. In attempt to fix or break our relationship.

"Sebastian, this is the third time you'd be leaving me!" she shouted. "Walk out that door again, and this will be the last time I ever go back with you." Her eyes were bathing in tears that were just a drop away from spilling over. She stood in front of me drained of her energy. Like a still zombie, waiting for my response.

And me confused if this was a decision I was willing to make. A woman's patience with a man can grow thinner than skin, and I knew this time around she was sure of her decision.

I was quiet for thirty seconds, but then I answered. "Okay that's fine with me…I'm done. It's over," I said.

The phrase was as cold as a sharp icicle. I could almost feel my words piercing through her chest as she sat down and buried her face in her palms. I have never heard her cry in such pain before. This image later in life had always crushed every part of my insides whenever I thought about it. I never felt good about what I did. She made a full payment with the value of her heart, when she bought the dreams that I had sold her.

I was avoiding the guilt, but it never made it disappear over time, and I proved myself wrong for thinking so. What I also learned through this life teaching was to never put another woman through such an upsetting situation again. There was no guideline or manual on how to love when I recklessly entered the relationship. It's not that I gave up, I gave out. I took the easy way out when I just left her. And being within the surroundings of the wrong influences was of no help either.

To be aware that there exists a woman out there that can use her experience with me as a lesson. On who and what type of man to avoid. It's not part of a story that I'm pleased that I played a role in.

Mike interrupted my thinking, my remembering. "You had trust issues that you might have brought into the relationship, bro…"

"I did. She just didn't have the eyes to see the wall I had up that she kept running into," I said.

Mike rolled down the window and started staring at the house, along with me. "You know how hard it is for a woman to take back a man that had left her in the first place?" he asked.

I had no answer as my body slumped while I just sat there. Feeling every bit of that question as it sunk in, slowly like a knife cutting through a cake.

Mike exhaled while nodding to my demeanor. "I'm sorry you feel that way, bro," he added.

"Yeah, well. I don't plan on using this regret as just weight on my shoulders. It should be more like the skates on my shoes to help me move different." I then continued, "At the end of the day I know now to have a little more respect for women in general."

Mike looked at me confused, understanding something else. "So you're single? And what now? You're going to just wait around?" he questioned.

"No, bro, just let me take things easy," I aggressively answered. "You only talked to those girls at the coffee shop. Because I practically forced you to prove to me you still got it," he added.

Yeah, and you saw how that turned out!" I shouted.

"Whatever, forget about that. And hey, if things don't work out it's cool. Keep it moving, I just don't want to see you like this," he mentioned.

My phone started to ring. It was Old Man Rich, calling to inform us that he will be out of town soon, but will let us know who will contact us on our work at his business. Some work we had set in a computer shop, for later this week.

As soon as I was off the phone, I felt the laser of someone's eyes cooking on the side of my head. I was quick to notice that inside the old house we were parked in front of, there was someone who stared out the window. I didn't want them calling the cops reporting us being suspicious. So I hit Mike on the shoulder. "Hey, let's get out of here before those people think we are wanting to break in or something," I warned.

We rushed out of there, speeding once he noticed what I had pointed out.

Some of our choices are a mistake, but we don't know that until time defines it as a mistake later on. Later on, also meaning too late. No matter how it's approached, you can only learn from the things you cannot fix. There's no way to circle around that. For every man unaware and ungrateful of his good woman, there's a guy such as myself and others who regrets the loss of her. To get drafted to us is easy, but not a team that another man would ever want to join.

CHAPTER 3

An Unexpected Guest in My Life

I found her, but she lost me. I found her so attractive, that she lost me on how to explain it.

Three days had gone by since we were sitting in front of the old house I had rented out with Isabel. And here we were. Mike and I had put up the Sheetrock in Old Man Rich's computer repair store. A customer we had done business with several times. The store was closed because of our remodeling. All we had to do was paint the walls on the other half of the store and also put the carpet in. On the corner room that was soon to be available for more space, meaning more room for equipment to be sold, for a second our eyes were too busy wandering at the photos in Rich's office. Then we just happened to come across a sketch, in which we both put our attention to.

"I've tried but I could never do that," said Mike as he was flick-ing his fingers on the sketch. "Draw someone's face like it's a photo with the shades and color of just a pencil." There was a white sheet of paper on the wall, over the computer. With Rich's face drawn on it. Which looked very detailed. He appeared to be laughing in the sketch, as if enjoying a holiday dinner with family. Right underneath in dark letters it was signed dad, which led me to assume, and also explain to Mike. "You might not be able to draw like that. But it looks like his daughter knows what she is doing with that pencil," I added.

"You think that was his daughter?" he questioned.

"It has to be, he never mentioned having a son."

"You have a point there Sebastian," he agreed with me. There were pictures of a gorgeous tropical queen, with an art to her curves, giving her a goddess appearance. Scattered all over Rich's office, many in which she was hugging Rich tight enough to squeeze the eyes out of his sockets. But only one in particular caught my attention, as well as my breath. I pushed some cardboard boxes out of my way with my feet as I approached. Leaned in and softly placed my fingers on the edges of the picture. Slowly I whispered under my breath to myself, "She's beautiful." In the picture she was sitting on a sofa with her legs crossed, elbow on the armrest, chin sitting on her hand and looking away. Wearing a forest green dress with sand-color shoes. The only picture where I didn't see her smiling. But it was still gorgeous to me. It captured a different type of beauty, I would say. With her jet-black hair and caramel skin.

I broke my focus when I felt Mike staring at me while he stood aside me. "You need a napkin for drooling?" mumbled Mike, with sarcasm.

"You and your jokes," I replied, annoyed.

"I like this picture. I don't know why, but I do."

"It's because she's by herself," assumed Mike.

"No, not at all," I assured him.

I suddenly felt Mike's arm go around my shoulders as he pointed at the whole wall of pictures. "You should ask to meet her," he suggested.

"What? Ask Old Man Rich to see his daughter? Nah, man. How does that look?" I argued.

"It looks like you're just being friendly! But okay, well, anyways this weekend we are going out somewhere. Because you have to get out more," he demanded.

I had no intentions on getting out more. But I was getting in more, on my curiosity of this woman. I started to dwell on what was going to be my approach. I've always known that beauty is common. There's plenty of beautiful women out there, and there's more to know about an individual than just that. In society everything looks more of value with a model in it. A posting of a car show, a celebrity on the red carpet with his date, even the ringside girls who hold up the signs displaying the upcoming rounds in a boxing match. The surface of a person looks appealing to the eyes. What man doesn't love to have a beautiful woman in his arms? If she's a ten on the outside and the low score of a three on the inside. You'll be sleeping with a ten, but your differences will be battling with this low level of a three. So I wasn't thinking of love at first sight. I was curious about who she was and what she was about. And wanted to start the process on getting to know her. We heard keys jingling at the front door and a squeak as the door opened.

"That's Rich… Let's tell him we'll be back tomorrow," I said to Mike as footsteps approached.

"Guys, are you there?" yelled Rich. Then he suddenly caught us coming out his office.

"Hey, Rich!" I interrupted while I stepped in his path. "All the Sheetrock is up. We also took care of the broken wood and trash left in the basement. How does tomorrow sound to do the painting?" I asked.

He looked around, impressed, and smiled. "Good! And about the floor?"

Mike then intervened: "We will also put the carpet in tomor-row. It should be all set, Rich."

He shoved his hand into his pocket and pulled out some money to hand to me. "Here, from what I had owed you two."

"Thank you. And hey, Rich. You are not going to be here, right?" I was confirming with him, as he took a second to clear his throat before he answered.

"Yes, about that. I was searching to find someone to be here for me. And also check up on you guys in case you two are in need of anything. Finally, my daughter told me that she could do me the favor," explained Rich. His face was as still as a wall, eyes dead on my face before he informed me. "Her name is Valerie," he firmly said. More than likely she meant the universe to him. Not just the world, that would be just a fragment according to his demeanor.

"No problem, Rich," I assured him. I leaned in to shake his hand and also commented to him closely, "Family is always there when we need them."

"Yes, especially her. Man, I can always count on that kid." He sighed then calmly strolled into his office to go through e-mails, and shut the door. We started packing our power tools and getting ready to wrap things up, just another day of work at its end.

"Are we going to the gym today?" Asked Mike, exhausted.

"I'm not sure. I can't wait to get out of these work boots. I'll think about it once I'm home."

"No way! Mr. Muscle Head says no to the gym?" mentioned Mike, surprised.

"Every now and then, it's good to take a few days off in a row. I'm still sore from last time," I confessed. Mike took a glance at the office door, which remained shut for the moment. He pulled me away to break down one of his dumb relationship techniques that he had suddenly put together, but I hope he'd never perform it in the real world.

"Listen closely please," he started to detail his techniques to me. "Soon as you start dating a girl, try your best to woo her. Seduce the hell out of her, have her blindly in love with you… Right?" whis-pered Mike, with a sharp stare and a smile underneath it. I crossed my arms and focused my ears, awaiting for the purpose of this all. "And when you are so sure she's in a floating cloud infatuated over you, you dump her!" he blurted.

I jumped up confused as to why he would say this. "And what the hell is that supposed to do?" I shouted.

"Think about it," he said, with his hand lightly resting on my shoulder. "She's going to wonder why, without a sign or a fight did, you do such a thing. She'll beg for forgiveness of the unknown and desire you more!" he said excitedly.

I paused and took offense to the idea. "And that's it? Hurt her and forget her?" bothered, I questioned him.

"Well no, you take her back. But she'll see you as unpredictable and will be more likely to behave!" he assured me I wasn't sure if this was one of his sarcastic jokes digging for a reaction. Or if Mike actually meant what he said. Either way, I felt I had to give my advice. "Don't you ever do that. That's exactly how you create a psycho out of a woman," I warned him. But since he shared a horrible tactic assuming it may work, I took it as an oppor-tunity to share with him a much better one. "Hey, you know I under-stand the feeling. Nice breasts, nice legs, looks so good right? But I don't care how much you desire a body. Mike that body has a per-sonality, a mind, a soul. That body belongs to a person, in this case a woman. So be the best man you can be, to the woman she is. And you never know, Mike, that woman might just surrender her body to you," I explained. "Not that crap you just said!" I added, shouting.

As he laughed off his idea, he glanced at the office door again, and suddenly he changed the conversation. "Hey, man, you saw how Old Man Rich just looked at you serious when he mentioned his daughter?" recalled Mike. "He knows she's hot! So he's being all pro-tective," he mocked.

"Nah, man. They're probably just really close. Can your Dominican ass ever assume something else?" I joked.

"Yeah, well, anyways, can your Puerto Rican ass buy the coffee and breakfast tomorrow?" he argued back.

Mike is this six-foot-one Dominican American, who thinks highly of himself at times and is always in a playful mood. Him being just a few inches taller than me, if it was not short jokes once in a while, it was usually something else that he felt he had over me. He'd feel I could be too serious at times, the same way I felt he could tone down his sarcasm a bit. We'd had our big differences, but we've been friends long enough now. I did owe us breakfast this time around too, and there was no arguing there.

CHAPTER 4

Valerie Is Her Name

They can tell you to smile, I rather be the one to find you a reason to smile.

Most people in Massachusetts, when they see rain in the forecast, they frown. Changing their mood, along with their daily activities. Counting the days or hours that it eventually passes by diminish and leave. I have always thought of it under a different shade of think-ing. The tune that the rainfall makes is enough calming music to sooth any cloudy mind. And watching it fall is just as relaxing. That is exactly what kind of day we are waking up to. The smell of fresh coffee was hovering all inside the truck after Mike and I had finished breakfast headed to Rich's store.

"It's almost 8:00 a.m. man, I hope she's there already," Mike mumbled, appearing half asleep still.

Taking my time down streets covered by streams of water, I drove in silence and said nothing in response. About twenty min-utes later, we were carefully rolling the truck into the heavy, soaked parking lot. "Looks like the lights are on," I pointed out to Mike. "Someone has to be there," I then assured.

The carpets and padding were left inside yesterday. All we had to bring in were the tools, paint, rollers, and brushes.

A female figure approached the door as we were preparing to exit the truck. "Whenever you're ready, I'll open the door!" shouted

Valerie as she stuck her head out and back in the door in a peekaboo fashion.

"Sebastian, we have two trips so let's make this quick!" shouted Mike.

We were partially soaked by the time we were settled inside. Valerie was holding an umbrella, rushing to leave. She carried the same beauty in person as in the pictures, the jet-black hair com-bined with the shine of her caramel skin. And her curves were still artistically displayed even through her raincoat, which was wrapped around her gorgeous self.

"Hey, guys, my dad told me about the work you guys had to do in the store."

"Yes, we do," I declared.

"I'm sorry but I have to go, but I will be back here later. If there's anything you guys need, the number to reach me at is on the desk in the office," she informed us.

I didn't need the use of her number just yet. Just as much as I didn't expect such a fast encounter. But we did have work to do. And it was best to get busy now, and catch her at a time when she was not in such a hurry.

Four hours had gone by. The painted walls made the room look brighter, the new carpet adding to the life of the store.

"She didn't even introduce herself," argued Mike.

"We shouldn't take it personal. We don't know exactly what was the reason or state of mind she could be in," I explained.

"And it's okay, there's enough time for that," I finished saying.

He looked me up and down, becoming even more impatient. "Time?" he blurted, with his eyes almost pushing out of his skull. "I think our time is up, we should get going. To top it off, it stopped raining," he argued. I grabbed the broom and ignored the hell out him, then proceeded sweeping away the debris in the store. Suddenly from outside I heard a car pulling into the parking lot; it was Valerie. "Good, she's here," Mike sighed, relieved. He proceeded to pace around, thrusting the stuff we brought in, as he grabbed it all. He then stopped and turned toward me. "Um…you plan on talking for a while with this chick? Or are we leaving right away? Just let me know what to expect," he demanded.

I had a gift card in my wallet that I haven't used. I pulled it out and held it in front of Mike, in hopes of him grasping what I was about to teach. "Sometimes, my friend, it's not all about what you say. It's also what you do," I promised him.

Valerie rushed in the door, although it was a fast pace, and she was still breathing heavy. She did appear to be more laid back than when we first saw her. "Hey, guys! Sorry I left in such a hurry I—" she silenced herself. And took the moment to look around the store. "Oh! Looks a lot better, thank you! My dad will be happy with this," she said.

I lowered my tone and spoke to her softly. "Your welcome, Valerie."

She smiled, and completely relaxed was her breathing. "I'm sorry for not introducing myself. I'm Valerie, it's just that I was in a rush," she explained.

"And I'm Mike! That's my best friend Sebastian," interrupted Mike, looking like a happy child.

"Well, Valerie, the store is all yours now. We will talk to your dad soon about the work," I assured.

Changing the mood in the room, I lowered my tone again and intimately stepped in close to her. "Hey, listen, your dad and I were talking about food. And I know he's a steak lover," I said.

"Oh god, yes he is," she gushed.

"Well this is a gift card to Jimmy Jim's Steakhouse. They have the best steak I've ever tasted. I forgot to mention this spot to your dad," I added. "But hey, I know he's been busy and he can use a break. Maybe dinner with his daughter," I suggested. Her face was wrinkled with confusion, with her hand placed on her hip.

"Whenever is the next time you two spend family time together. I know how important that can be," I explained.

Her eyes grew, and her jaw hung a bit in surprise as to why would I be so nice. "Wow, um, thank you! That's so nice of you." She accepted. Flipping the card over and observing it, she wondered, "Does my dad have any clue about this?"

"No, not at all. And don't tell him," I demanded. "Just surprise him, take him out, and don't tell him where you got the idea. I'm telling you he's going to love the steak there, everyone does! And I'm aware he's never been to this one in particular," I said.

She looked down at the card, almost ashamed to accept. "There's enough on that card to serve dinner for two and a bot-tle of wine if desired," I also added.

The corners of her eyes were smiling, her lips slightly frowning but with joy. "I can't wait to take him there now," she promised. The short time that we spoke, Mike was already in the truck waiting for me. I walked off after saying goodbye, but I could sense her eyes watching my every step. You can hear a mouse walk, as quiet as it was. I rushed to the truck once I was outside. Sat down quickly and gazed down at my lap, smiling about my own ideas. "You gave her your number, right?" questioned Mike.

"And why would I do that? No, I didn't," I confessed. "But I did leave our business card on the keyboard in the office."

His face slowly turned into a raisin wondering why. But as soon as I broke down what happened in there, he came to realize. That this gesture had the potential to drive her to eventually reach out to me. "Oh I see what you did. You think your slick, huh?" said Mike. He then grew curious. "What are you going to say to Rich?"

"That's the easiest part. I'm glad you asked. I'm going to tell him this was all your idea!" I said, while I shoved my finger in his chest.

"Hell no, that's your issue," he argued.

I laughed and brushed it off. I then looked over at the store, just to notice Valerie's backside as she walked away from the door. She must have been watching us this whole time we were parked. Mike started up the truck, and as we exited the lot, I answered his question. "I'm not planning on saying a thing. I'm just going to let time tell us everything."

CHAPTER 5

A Date to Remember

I'd rather die of laughter than live a long life of misery

A week had gone by since Mike and I had left Old Man Rich's store. Home improvement was our primary work. But we did everything else a handyman can do, including mechanic work.

We had just finished putting in a brand-new muffler in a friend's car. He had left us with the vehicle in his driveway while he was off to go work his shift.

"Are we adding this to the scrap-metal pile?" wondered Mike about the old muffler.

"Yes, of course! Why would you ask?" I shouted, as I hovered over the old muffler, reaching to grab one end. "Let's throw it in the pickup for now," I suggested to Mike.

My phone started to ring while I adjusted the muffler in the bed of the truck. "Hey, man, try to position this while I answer my phone," I demanded. I picked up only to hear silence for a moment, but then: "Sebastian?"

"Yes?"

"You were right," said Valerie, in a tone rich with excitement. "My dad completely fell in love with the steak at the restaurant. Thank you," she gushed.

As happy as she was to please her dad, it was exactly how I felt to hear from her. "Good!" excitedly, I replied. "That's going to be his new spot now, I bet," I added.

"Yes! We were only halfway through our food. And he was already planning on when to make another visit," she recalled.

My lips had slowly curled into a smile while I listened to her discuss about how impressed her dad was. Once she took a peaceful pause, I softly added, "If only I knew what's your favorite restaurant. I'd be more than happy to take you there."

She went silent as soon as she heard me. But then with shy-ness filling her voice she shifted the conversation a bit. "Um…well, I called you to say thank you. And that was very nice of you, it meant a lot," she confessed.

I wasn't sure why she was avoiding a possible date with me, but since I didn't get a no for an answer, I wasn't going to stop just yet. "You're very welcome Valerie. And do you know of any private investigators?" I teased.

"No, why would you ask that?"

"because we need all it takes to figure out what's your favorite restaurant," I said sarcastically.

She tried to hold back her laughter. But the unexpected sarcasm made her only last two seconds before she burst out giggling. "So you're asking me out on a date, huh?" she mumbled.

I continued to tease since I felt that her comfort level had increased over the phone, as I was even more comfortable myself. "It could be worse. I could be asking for your address, but that would be too creepy," I said, as she chuckled a bit.

"Yeah, that sounds like too much. But okay, how 'bout this," she replied, laughing. "I'll think about it, and I'll call you tomorrow morning with my decision."

I gave the thought a quick scan across my mind. "If you call me too early, Valerie, I might ask you what's your favorite place for breakfast," I teased some more.

She giggled then rushed me off the phone. "Bye, Sebastian, we'll talk tomorrow," she gushed then hung up.

This was a special woman. And I could feel it all through my body, down to every standing hair on my skin whenever I talked to her. To know that I haven't felt like this in ages. Had me feeling like this life of mine was making sense all over again. Tomorrow couldn't come sooner. I was anxious for today to hurry up and vanish already. So I could take the first steps in this new journey.

After hanging up, I went back to getting my tools together since the old muffler part was already in the truck. Sweat was stinging the cuts on my forearm done from torn parts of the muffler.

"Here's a wet towel," Mike said, trying to help. "And who was that on the phone? I saw how fast you walked away," he said. I was happy to announce to Mike about Valerie and the possibility of a date. "That's good news! Now you're not scaring me anymore. Not so long ago, I thought I was going to lose you to loneliness," he clowned as he gave me a hard pat on the back.

"Yeah, well, things don't happen when you want them to hap-pen. I'm dating now," I mentioned. I walked away from him with a smile.

"Sebastian, this is just one woman out of many out there," he argued as he followed behind me with the tool bag.

"Yeah, but…what if I just won? The woman, that you say is just one woman. But she really is the one, this woman? And all I need. Either way we will have to see. And I'm willing to make that discov-ery," I said, before I snatched the tool bag from his hand and placed it in the bed of the truck.

Even though my first sight of her was in pictures, I felt robbed of my lungs, the way she took my breath away. We know that every body part plays its part, even though our feet are used to walk and our mouths to eat and talk. She did not need her hands when she grabbed me with her smile. Now anything can happen at this point; things can go left, or they can go right. Though my main intentions are not like a massage with a happy ending. But if we end up together happy, there shouldn't be no ending.

Early in the morning I received a surprise call after coming out the shower. I picked up the phone, still wrapped in my towel. It was Valerie. "Hello? I didn't think you would call this early," I responded, surprised.

"Good morning, Sebastian. Is 7:00 a.m. too early?" she asked.

"No, no, it's not. I see you made your decision early," I added.

"About that!" excitedly, she started. "I know you were joking about breakfast. But that's actually not a bad idea, especially at this time," she suggested.

I have to admit, she caught me off guard with the request. And there was no way I was to turn it down. "Well, there's a diner close to your dad's store. I can be there in an hour if you'd like to meet," I said.

"Yes! That's a good idea, I'll see you there," she assured. I wanted to be seated by the time she arrived. So I made it there a few minutes early, sitting where I could see her soon as she pulled into the parking lot, and also easy for her to spot me once she walked in. I wrote a few questions on a piece of paper and left it visible on the table. Questions I would later ask on this breakfast date.

I saw her park and get out of her car. It was probably quick, but in the way I saw it she stepped out in slow motion. My eyes enjoy-ing the satisfying movements of her calm body language. That natu-ral caramel complexion, and even from a distance her jet-black hair would shine. And was so soft on my eyes, as it would feel to touch, I could imagine. Once she walked in, she spotted me immediately. The look of a familiar face in her eyes followed by a growing smile in slow motion. The rhythm of her shoes tapping as she walked in my direction was like the song to her sexy walk.

"Sorry, I didn't put on makeup," she joked. She had the face of a doll that didn't need makeup anyways; I was sure she was aware of that as well.

"I don't think you need the chemicals of makeup on your face, by the way," I said. She put on a full smile and looked away quickly. "But honestly the worst makeup you can wear is a frown on your face, and I can already see you smiling. Such a healthy behavior," I flirted.

She slid the tip of her tongue back and forth, on the back of her bottom lip, thinking to herself it appeared. "There's something about you, and I'm going to figure it out soon," she determined.

"That's fine with me. But first let's figure out what your tummy wants, and we go from there," I suggested. We both ordered our food. I moved the piece of paper from the middle of the table, to under the syrup holder in the corner. And since I had placed the paper on the table with the questions not visible, she didn't get a glance yet of what this was.

"So what made you change your mind?" I asked.

"I figured I'd give you less time to think. While hoping to sur-prise you," she confessed.

"I'm not big on surprises, Valerie, but since I'm myself all the time, I don't fear it either," I claimed with confidence. I then fol-lowed with a question, "And if it's okay, can you surprise me with a little about yourself?"

She tilted her head and pressed her lips into a smirk, while her eyes went small like she was looking through a fog. "If you should know, I am twenty-seven, no kids, Hawaiian, originally from California, a high school poetry teacher," she detailed, followed by some humor. "Who for some reason is sitting here with this strange man."

It did accomplish some laughter out of me. "Wow, you sur-prised me with the teacher thing. Poetry, huh? My interest just grew a bit," excitedly, I added.

"And what about you? Other than I know you're very busy building houses."

I laid my hands flat in front of her and began to describe. "I'm a handyman all around. I enjoy all the tough work, no kids either. I've done mostly construction-based jobs since I was young. I'm eight years older than you, by the way," I detailed. She had this unsure look on her face, so I asked if it was my confession about my age.

"No, not at all," she assured me. "You're not that much older or old at all. I usually just don't go on a date with a muscular man such as yourself. And this is no offense, I just have a different type," she confessed.

I moved my glass of orange juice from in front of me and whis-pered closely, "I feel special then" and smiled.

Our food had arrived as we had normal chatter in between our meals then moments after we ate, as we were still enjoying our share of words. Until it all started to feel empty, as I call it. I determined to make it interesting when she asked me, "So what's your favorite color?"

"I don't have one," I said, while I rolled my eyes. She was staring at me, shocked, and I could tell she wasn't buying it, so I explained, "If you look at a masterpiece painting, and you observe it, the painter finds his own way to put all the colors into its beautiful form. If the painting is good, all the colors involved are beautiful."

"Yes, but you still should have a favorite color," she demanded me to answer.

In a dull tone of voice, I answered, "Well, Valerie, if you must know…it's blue." As I confessed, I had a smirk on my face, and my eyelids were low.

"Why would something so simple be so complicated?" she asked.

"This is the way I see it, questions such as 'What's your favorite color?' 'Do you like ice cream?' They just don't have much substance to them. They describe very little even about the surface of a person," I explained.

She leaned back quickly and crossed her arms. "What do you mean?" she wondered.

I reached for the paper I wrote on before she got here. She saw me pulling it out and placing it in front of her.

"I was going to ask you what was that when I had just sat down," she mentioned.

"Read it," I told her. "But read it out loud to me. And then answer the questions."

Slowly she grabbed the paper and flipped it over. Her eyes opened wide with a look of sarcasm. "Really? Three questions and ironically look at the first one. Hmm…okay," impressed, she added.

"Go ahead, read it," I suggested.

"Sure, here we go. Instead of asking what's our favorite color, why don't we ask what color do we think favors the other person." She placed the paper down on the table and pondered in a daze as she stared at my shirt. "I would have to say gray and black," she answered.

I have to say that even though I do like gray I still had to ask why she chose those colors, and here were her reasons: "Honestly I think you look good in gray, even a little sexy."

I laughed in reaction to her compliment. "I'm glad you think so… and why black?" I asked.

She took a sip of her orange juice while she pondered the question. "I chose black because that mysterious look in your eyes makes me feel that there is more to you," she explained.

"Okay, I can accept that," I responded. I tapped on the paper and told her to continue reading.

"Question number two: when was the last time that you heard of a fact that shocked you?" She pondered briefly, and suddenly excited, her voice went high pitched. "Oh my god! There was a case of a guy that had died from laughter! At first I didn't think that would ever be something that's even possible. But then again, the pressure of the laughter could have triggered cardiac arrest or something," she explained, then added, "it was labeled as a rare form of death when I read it of course."

I myself was surprised to hear the news of such a thing. I was as shocked as she was when she learned that. With so many different ways there is to leave this earth, that has to be the happiest way out.

Adding to the material for good conversation, I shared my thoughts on it. "Wow that's news to me, I guess you're not even safe having a good time," I joked. "I'm going to have to look that one up just in case you're lying to me," I teased.

She put her hand on my forearm and promised me it was a fact. "I'm not lying, and go ahead look it up! I believe it was some time last year," she recalled.

I could tell she was feeling a bit more comfortable, as I didn't expect that she would break the touch barrier at this point.

I then continued with the subject. "Well, whoever that guy was, I'll tell you one thing: he died happy. And that right there just inspired me to come up with a new life quote," I said.

"Really? Well let me hear it, what's the quote?" excited she asked. As I stared softly into her eyes, I whispered, "I'd rather die of laughter than live a life of misery."

She sits back and looks at the table while she smiled, and the peace in her demeanor was that of a forest with ancient trees. I noticed her in a daze. Going into her own thoughts, I decided to snap her out of it. "I don't think we are done!" I shouted, awaking her from the daydreaming she was having.

"Oh yeah? There's another question. You are right." She flipped the paper and went to read the next. "Question number three: can you recall the last time your laughter of an incident was so strong, that your stomach cramped up, your breath went very short, and tears were slowly pushing out of your eyes?" She seemed to have no problem claiming what incident right away as she exploded giggling just to the thought of it.

"Oh my god! Give me a second." She chuckled and then started with the incident. "My dad, one day when I was over his house, was sitting in his chair having an amazing conversation with me. And the cat he used to have that he called Cocoa…" She stopped and laughed for a second, disrupting her own story. "Sorry…anyways Cocoa jumped on his lap, and dad was calm petting the cat and talking to me. All of a sudden he jumped in the air!" She shouted, while putting a hand over her mouth briefly. "The cat and him were in midair along with a dead mouse!" she finished saying, as she cov-ered her mouth again and laughed with her face and neck that had turned bright red.

I attempted to finish the story for her. "Oh I see, the cat killed a mouse and brought the trophy to his master who apparently freaked out?" I assumed.

With her other hand waving air in her face, she nodded. She expressed how funny his demeanor was, how she was confused from the outburst until she saw the mouse. And she went as far as imi-tating her dad's reaction and swearing. It was beautiful to watch her happy face express a moment in her life of a good time. Good con-versations are usually intellectual, but a good laugh serves its purpose as well. And instead of guessing what might be funny to a person you don't know completely just yet, why not remind them of something they already had a good time laughing with? In other words, all my questions had its reasons why I chose them to be on the list. But what I wasn't expecting was her putting her own twist to this game of questions.

"But…I do have a question for you," she added. "I don't know, it's kind of random I guess," she mumbled, while roaming her eyes on the back of the paper.

I was anxious to know, and therefore I demanded her to ask. "Go ahead! I like the fact that you're playing along."

"Okay…I want to put my own creativity to this," she explained. Her emotional pause led me to believe that this question was coming from a sensitive place inside her. "If you have ever been a person who has been hurt before because of love, then it would be no surprise if you're afraid to love again. Your fear of falling for someone would be understandable."

I nodded and let her finish.

"But what if you met someone that you yourself fell for? But this person is the one who is afraid to fall for you? How would you handle that?" she asked.

I didn't think the question was an easy one to answer. Since con-vincing a person who's been hurt that you're not here to cause them any harm, they might just have to lose that fear first before they can move on. And before they can even accept your true intentions.

After a moment of pondering, I gave her my answer. "That's a good one. Because you can possess the exact true love indicated for this person. But like a dying patient refusing the right blood dona-tion if they refuse who is for them because they haven't healed, for-given, and so on. There's not much we can do," I finished saying.

She nodded, thinking, then started to play with her keys. "Thank you for breakfast, and for the talk. You think we could do this another time?" she wondered.

This woman felt so warm to me without feeling her whole body. How could I say no to such a request? I accepted, paid the bill, and walked her to her car. Tomorrow is another day, or should I say another adventure in this journey with Valerie. The smile she left on me kept sneaking up on my face whenever she came to mind. If I closed my eyes for a second, the looks she gave me at the table were right in my vision. Echoes of her pleasing laugh would breeze through my ears. Her caramel skin and her soft hair napping on her shoulders with the edges hanging off.

The surprise of her adding a question to the list I presented to her was an act that let me know she was a woman of involvement. Involved in a man's intent, progressions, and possibly livelihood. A woman not afraid to set her own helpful opinion. I also found her careful approach to me attractive. Not shy but cautious with me, which was of no bother since I didn't have a thing to hide. Just happy with our date was a shallow way to describe how I felt about it. I was more than ready for the next time out with her.

CHAPTER 6

An Accident Off Guard

We know that actions speak louder than words. But it's the actions of our eyes, having words together, that speak even louder.

"So what do you think, Sebastian? This looks like a lot of work," asked Mike.

We were both in a customer's basement debating what to charge him to fix the floor. There was plenty of damage to the concrete that he left for us to repair. Severe damage to the whole basement con-crete, from corner to corner.

"Well, my friend, we are going to need our grinding blade, circular saw, and maybe chisels and hammer as well," I suggested to Mike.

He jerked his neck and shouted in despair. "You crazy? This is like the whole basement! Look how deep those cracks are. We'll need a jackhammer for most of this," he argued.

"You're right…and don't forget about the cement mix we'll have to buy and charge him for," I said, with my voice heavy and head hurting from acknowledging what we had to work on.

We sat down for a moment to contemplate this project. I changed the subject briefly to sooth our minds. "Hey, man, I'm thinking of what to wear or where to go when Valerie and I decide when our second date will take place," I mentioned.

Mike turned his face to ask. "You really like this girl huh?" he said. "She doesn't seem the type to get impressed easy, you have a plan or what?" he asked.

I rolled my eyes and raised my voice. "Of course, man! You should know me by now, whenever I'm serious about something. It's a 95 percent chance it will be mine. I would say higher, but I'll give that 5 percent to God, in case he feels different about my path," I said.

Mike looked away and started to smile at the wall. It made me wonder what the gesture was about, and I grabbed him by the shoulder and turned him back to me. "What? What was that? You want to mention something, don't you?" I aggressively asked.

He raised his hands and gave in. "Okay, okay! I have something to tell you."

"What is it?" I asked, confused.

"Remember the two girls at the coffee shop we met that time?"

"Yes."

"Well, I started talking to Lisa," he confessed.

Thinking I might not have heard him correctly, I asked, "Wait a minute. Lisa? Lisa is the girl that was supposed to have been talking with me, right?" I recalled.

"Yes. That's the one. I finally called them and…well, you know, we are supposed to go grab a drink somewhere soon. I mean you don't like 'em married, so hey! More fun for me," he bragged.

I didn't care one bit about the woman; I wasn't interested in another man's wife. But this switch-up did catch me off guard. I now had a woman much more important to me to discover about. But I was still happy to encourage Mike to do as he pleased. "Hey, do you, Mike? I just didn't expect you two to hit it off," I confessed. "How did that come about?" I asked.

"Long story. I'll break it down when I can," he assured me.

At that moment we stood up from being seated and decided to clear the floor a bit from all the stuff around. There was a bag filled with soccer balls we had to move across to the other end for now. Behind it was trash and a twenty-four-by-fifty-two-inch window cut that was to be thrown out.

"Sebastian, take the glass. I'll take this trash bag, and let's go outside," he asked, while helping me.

"Hand me the glass," I asked him, since he stood right in front of it.

Underestimating its weight, I reached with one arm only. My hand was still slightly moist from sweat I wiped off my forehead moments ago. The glass slipped off my hand. When the sharp edge hit my leg, I just realized that this time around I had boots with jean shorts. Out of all days I had to wear shorts today. Nothing in the way of this glass to cause it some friction at the least. The edge plunged through my flesh and muscle. I felt a tear and a snap, and I grabbed the glass with both hands and pulled it off quickly.

"Oh! Sebastian!" yelled Mike as he grabbed the glass away from me. I stood there and looked down at my shin with a chunk of meat just hanging. I could see bone and muscle. I wasn't dizzy, but for some reason my leg buckled, and I fell seated on the ground.

"Damn that looks bad! We have to get you to the hospital" yelled Mike in a panic to get me upstairs and out of the house.

I suddenly felt some numbing as it settled In. "It feels weird, bro, I can't move my foot much," I explained.

"Don't worry, I'll carry you to the truck. Damn it! Let me grab something to wrap up your leg before we leave!" he shouted.

He grabbed some clean rags that were sitting on a pile of folded clothes on top of the washer in the basement. All I cared about at that moment was to stop the bleeding and get to the hospital. Mike wrapped my leg up and tied some strings around to keep it in place.

"Damn, Mike, half my foot is tingling," I complained to him. "Man! Let's get out of here! I have to get this checked!" I was screaming my words in pain.

"Calm down, man, give me your hand. I'll have to carry you to the truck," he said. Then he helped me get upstairs and outside. Right then and there the owner of the house pulled into the driveway.

"Oh my god what happened?" he blurted out in a panic as he approached us with his hands trembling.

"Your glass fell on his leg and cut him deep," explained Mike. "And he needs to get to a hospital. We will talk some other time about the basement," Mike assured him.

Just in case he was afraid of a lawsuit of some sort, I went on and added, "Don't worry, it's not your fault."

He chuckled then sighed as if relieved that I had said that. Now I was sitting in the truck worried. How did I let this happen? And how long would it be until I could work again? That was just a few worries out of many that I had in mind. For active individuals such as myself, being physically unable to function is a nightmare we never want to accept in our smallest of dreams. Both Mike and I were quiet during the speedy ride to the hospital. As my friend, he knew how strong I felt about the situation. He felt my agony and let me crumble in emotional pain while I sat there in my own little world. Although Mike loved to clown around a lot, he knew when the situ-ation was serious.

We arrived at the hospital, and they took me in immediately. I was happy to be stitched up. But this loss of motion still bothered my mind. "Doc I don't know, but my leg feels odd," I informed him.

His forehead wrinkled. "What do you mean exactly?" "I can't move my foot that much," I explained as I sat on the hospital bed with my legs dangling.

He wheeled in on his little seat and asked me to place my heel on his palm. "Try to move your foot to the right," he asked. I did just that.

"Good! now move it to the left."

I then moved to the left.

"Good! Okay now with the ball of your front foot, press down like you are pressing on a gas pedal."

I felt some pain, but I was still able to press down.

Then with a sure look on his face that we were about to find the problem, he asked. "Now I'm going to put my hand on the top of your foot. I want you to pull up with your foot."

I couldn't move my foot at all. I made several attempts and nothing.

The doctor looked up at me and exhaled. "Sir, I'll have to speak with one of the doctors for a moment. I believe you did more damage than just cut your leg," he explained, concerned.

I closed my eyes and sat there with my head down, expecting the worst. Anger with a mixture of sadness all swirled up into one emotion. Suddenly Valerie's eyes came into my mind. She told me a few things with her words when on our date, but a lot more with her looks and glances. I did not want her to see me like this, so I wasn't planning at all to contact her. It just made me feel calm inside to think about that woman. I needed a quick escape from this horrible situation.

As white as the floor was, it kept dimming to me in my vision. The room had a scary silence where all I could hear was the sound of my fingers digging on the bed's cushion, as I rocked back and forth dealing with my impatience alone.

After further evaluation, MRI and all, I find out that apart from flesh and muscle, I had cut the tendon that pulls my foot up. It cut off just a few inches up from my ankle, and the lower part had rolled into my foot causing it to swell up. They were going to have to bring both ends together and stitch them up. I was scheduled for surgery the very next morning.

CHAPTER 7

My Stay at the Hospital

I wish I can freeze those moments, in where I melt your heart...

I was awakened by the moans and groans of my neighbor in the room. My first sight was the ceiling. Surgery was over, but this pain in my leg was as new as the present moment. Before surgery the pain was only from the cut to the foot. Now this pain was screaming in agony from my knee to my toe, louder than my voice can reach. What the hell did those doctors do, beat my leg with a pipe? I won-dered. It was the middle of the night, and even though I was drugged up, I still had flashes of pain waking me up. With the feeling of playing twenty games of football, I was exhausted and drained. My eyes wandered around the room for a few minutes. Then the sleep suddenly crept up and sunk me in deep.

Opening my eyes at 8:00 a.m. I saw a nurse walk in to offer me breakfast. Hungry as can be, how could I not? Scrambled eggs with pancakes, which happened to be my favorite. I hovered my nose right above the eggs as the steam hit my nostrils. I was having a moment right before enjoying its every taste.

Halfway done with my breakfast, I heard boots stepping fast toward my side of the room. It was Mike. "Hey, man! Your looking happier already," he joked.

Downing my orange juice, I was smiling as I put my cup down, appreciating the visit. "Even though I hate hospitals, I love this breakfast in bed," I joked right back.

He grabbed a seat right by my side then informed me, "Old Man

Rich called me yesterday. He was telling me how he had some repairs at his house for us to look at."

"Well, that's a good surprise. We've never been to his house before," I recalled.

Mike agreed then continued, "I told him we couldn't do any of that right now because of what happened to you."

I closed my eyes and crossed my arms as I listened in peace. He went quiet for a moment before he asked, "Have you talked to Valerie at all?"

"No. I don't feel right. I look a mess here in the hospital. She's called, but I'm too embarrassed to answer," I confessed, lowering my head in shame of my situation.

With a worried stare and his body slightly slumped toward me, he tapped his fingers on my bed and advised me. "Call her, man, I know she meant something to you. I can tell," he described.

I was pleased to have met her of course, but I was already in a state that I wanted to be left alone or at least not seen in such a con-dition. Eventually I would have to reach out to her. I assured Mike I would do so soon, and I quickly changed the subject after that. "So how's the house holding up?" I asked.

Mike and I shared a house that we split into two apartments. And between the basement and the garage we had every machine and tool needed for our home-improvement work that we set out to search. Just us, although at times when we had enough work we reached out to a friend to assist us.

Without a worry to my question, he answered, "Good! Everything is taken care of. All that matters now, bro, is that you're okay and that you recover just fine," he added with concern.

After an hour of normal conversation, I was in a daze with my head down facing my lap, feeling helpless. I could tell that Mike could read my frustration. He smiled then looked at me and sug-gested, "Call Valerie. She might be wondering how you're doing. I'm going to head out, bro, but I'll check up on you later." He walked out in slow motion.

I started to rehearse in my mind what it was I would tell Valerie. A phone call was probably what she was expecting, but I had the idea to text her. And if this was how I was going to reach out, I decided I might as well make it sound as special as I possibly can. This was what

I sent her:

> You were probably expecting a voice with these words
> I'm texting. It wasn't on purpose that I missed your
> calls, I was still aiming at reaching out to you. And
> that's an aim I wasn't going to miss. By now I'm sure
> you heard how I tore my leg, and this tear also tore me
> up inside. I'm such an active person that this inability
> to function was eating me live. It wasn't that I didn't
> want to see your face, it was my dealings with this stress
> I didn't want your face to be seeing. We spoke about
> another date, and I didn't expect our next date to be
> a hospital visit. But when you have the time, I'd be
> happy to see you make an appear-ance. I'll text you
> where to find me in a few.

I sent her the info right after, wishing I was there to see her reaction when reading what I had sent. I smiled to myself and started flicking through the channels on TV. Hours flew by like a peaceful, soft breeze. I could leave in a few more hours, or I could spend one more stay. I looked down at my hand while I rubbed my stomach. I was feeling hungry again.

A concerned voice broke my attention when I heard "Sebastian?" It was Valerie in an ocean-blue suit with a small black pocketbook at hand. I didn't have to ask. I just knew that she was getting out of work and came to visit me.

She smiled and ended it with a quick frown right after. "I have to say that I'm the poetry teacher, and you're becoming one of my favorites. And you're not even in my class," she said softy and laughed as she conversed with me.

She sits down with a flirtatious wiggle in her neck. "No but what you say is cute sometimes, and romantic," she admitted.

I thanked her and changed the subject to her. "So how was work for you today? Or should I say the love of your life? Because I sense you love what you do."

"It was great! And that is correct, I do love what I do." She looked down at her pocketbook as she caressed her hair. "So...I brought you this get-well card. With something inside for you," she revealed.

I watched her as she pulled it out her pocketbook and handed it to me. Inside was a folded letter to which she explained to me as soon as I start to unfold it.

"That's a poem from one of my students. When I read your text, I had finished reading his poem a few minutes earlier. The con-tent reminded me of your text a bit. It's about pain. I want to know your feedback on it," she asked of me.

The writing was shaky, but I was able to read the whole page. It was more like lyrics, and this is what the young man wrote:

> A tear drops my eyes, but my but eyes don't want to open / my heart is in its grave and the dirt is frozen / spiritual decay means my soul is decom-posing/ trying not to sleep and pass away, but I just keep dozing / you only see the skies clear because your life is okay / I've always seen my skies gray / to me it's just another day / walking away from this game because it's the devil who wants to play / my soul went to leave, my shadow moved out of its way.

Slowly I put the paper down and raised my voice. "What the? My god this is depressing!" I shouted.

She had a big smile with wide open eyes the whole time. "He's creative, right? I know it's a little dark, but the pain is so deep. Almost how you expressed your pain. But darker…" she detailed.

I shook my head and just accepted the poem. "Well, I guess… if you want to put it like that. And…who is this kid?" I questioned.

She was delighted to answer. "His name is William. He's one of the best students I had in years. He's very quiet and to himself. It's hard to get the words out his mouth. But when his pen touches that paper, wow! I'll tell you, something like this comes out," she described.

Then she turned her attention to me, sitting her elbow on her palm with her finger on her temple, and she questioned: "So have you ever taken up poetry in high school?"

"No, I didn't, but I actually read a few books with great poems." "Really? What poets have you read?" curiously she asked, but I could barely remember high school to remember any of them books. "I'm not sure, I used to read a collection of various poets." I sighed as I shook my shoulders, signaling for a change in conversation.

"Can I ask you something, Sebastian?"

I leaned in with open ears. "Sure, what's up?" I asked with a face full of curiosity.

"You're a handsome man, and very masculine at that. I'm sure you don't need to talk much. So why is it you put so much work into what you say and do?" she questioned, as she posed like a sitting psychologist, awaiting my answer.

Yes, physical compliments are okay. To me it was not every-thing, but since she wanted to say the word handsome, I figured I would hand some advice.

"Well, Valerie, my smile will always rise up, but with old age eventually my face will drop down. And as for my body, when this figure is eventually disfigured, what do I have left? What will I be left with? My ideas and creativity, my understanding of people, my intelligence, and any skills I've acquired in life. I believe those things are what really defines our attractiveness. Don't you think?"

She nodded, impressed at my response. It was at that moment that I knew she would be in my company for a long time. I saw her take a glance at the clock in the room. "I know you have to go. I'll be out of here soon anyways. And trust me, I appreciate the visit," I gushed.

"You're very welcome, Sebastian, and hopefully there will be more encounters with us in the near future," she murmured. As she stood close to the bed, I reached for her hand then held it softly and assured her, "Oh trust me, Valerie. There will be."

Her showing me a smile on our first date meant the table talk was going well. Showing up to the hospital and appearing to be wor-ried shows a much deeper caring to me. When helpless and in need of people's comfort, the memory of whoever was around becomes a special memory to us emotionally.

And on her part, something special was going on as well. Liking me from the beginning was for sure a good thing. But slowly car-ing for me from the start would only pull her in faster and deeper. Without her even seeing it coming, and without me planning it either. It just becomes the ingredients of what destiny of a couple is made of.

CHAPTER 8

Home Sweet Home

EIn the fall season the leaves change colors, causing a beautiful sight to the environment. In the fall of me falling for you, the beautiful sight is yourself. Who colors my world, my environment.

When someone you care about passes away, it will take you some time to accept that they are gone. It will feel as if they are still with you on this earth. Until you get used to the feeling of not having them around.

But on the flip side of things, have you ever met someone that had you in disbelief that they existed in your life? Matching every-thing that you will ever need? How is it that this type of person is actually in your life right now? That's how I was slowly starting to feel about Valerie.

There I was in my garage sitting close to one of our tool cabi-nets. Going through the drawers. I was organizing the wrenches and wiping grease out of all the sockets. This was keeping me entertained and my mind off my leg.

As I took a break, I had a handful of sockets, which I placed on the ground, making a V shape. In my attempt to spell the name Valerie. I did the V and was done with the A, but before I could even start the L she called me, what a pleasant interruption.

"Hello, Sebastian?"

I dazed off for a second. Letting her sweet voice sing those sim-ple words in my ear, until I heard her say hello again and I finally responded. "You know, if I told you I was just thinking about you, you probably wouldn't have believed me," I confessed.

Even though I could not see her on the phone, I could feel that she was smiling on the other end. "And why is that?"

"Never mind. Anyways, I'm just here in my garage organizing. What are you up to?" I simply asked.

"Well, I was actually thinking of paying you a visit."

Out of reaction, I started fixing my shirt and pushed my hair flat. Which in any of this fixing wasn't going to change the way I looked by much at all. Nervously, I accepted. "Um…sure. I, I, I'm not up to much," I stuttered.

She chuckled at my nervousness. "What's the address? I'm already on the road, by the way." she asked, while I heard the wind from passing cars as she had her window down.

After giving her the address, I rushed off the phone to do something for her. Something she could take home to remember. I stared at a wood board the size of a medium painting. I was hit with many ideas, but just one sparked the brightest light in me. I went directly for my coin stash to dig out only the pennies and write out a meta-phor. Placing it on a stand that I quickly put together, out of broom-sticks and small rope, I filled the board with the pennies, spelling out these words: "All I've done was put my two cents in, and you received me with your million-dollar smile."

I figured this would be an impressive gift, even though there was not lots of money behind it. And even though literally it was worth pennies, isn't it the thought that counts as priceless?

Her car had suddenly pulled into the driveway. I pretended to be painting something. She could see straight at me since the garage door was wide open. Tapping her shoes in my direction with her seductive walk. "Don't tell me that you are a painter!" she shouted.

I smiled and signaled with my hand to stop before I was ready to show her my work. "I might be, maybe not as good as the pros, though. But wait." I glued the last penny to finish the last word. "Tell me what you think?" I asked as I waved her to come see.

She walked over calmly and turned into the painting to read it. She put her hands over her mouth while her eyes slid across the sentence. "Aw…who's that for?" she asked.

I don't say a word. I just looked right at her, blinked once, and paused my smile.

"Thank you! I love it, Sebastian," she said, with her cheeks fully blushing out of that caramel skin of hers.

"Hey, I appreciate the visit at the hospital. And especially the thought of the postcard. So…you gave me a postcard, I make you this board of true facts," I flirted.

She sarcastically shook her head and rubbed her pockets "Well…a million-dollar smile. But I'd be happier to have a few mil-lion dollars instead," she joked.

I attempted to make her feel better of not having millions as I leaned toward her and lowered my voice. "Neither of us are rich, but that doesn't mean that you are not rich in beauty inside and out," I seductively expressed.

Her eyes were glowing; her smile was stretched to its extent. "Sebastian? Where do you come up with this stuff?"

"Up? I don't come up with anything. I come down on you with everything I have." I flirted some more.

She giggled and tried to change the subject. "Okay. Stop it, Sebastian. So how long will you have the cast on?"

"A month or so," I answered. "And then I have to go through therapy. The cast is only there so that I don't move my foot around while the tendon is healing… I hate this process," I confessed with a face full of worry.

She grabbed my hand and caressed her thumb on it. "It's okay, this can happen to the best of us. By the time you know it, this will all be done. I'll support you as much as I can. I can see how much this has affected you," she comforted.

I felt so much better to hear her say such a thing. I just wanted to grab her and kiss her. I hid how I felt to hear that, but I could sense she knew how she made me feel.

As she shone her sight all around my garage, she then started to touch my tools. "So this is your office, I can see. Interesting. I could barely see the walls with all your equipment in here," she mentioned curiously.

"It was all over time. Even though I do have a lot of tools and gadgets that we've had since the start," I explained.

I didn't want to feel as if I was boring her with the garage, so I invited her out. "Do you drink wine at all?" I asked.

She bit her lip and rolled her eyes. "I love wine." "Well, there is a nice vineyard that I've been to before that I think you might enjoy," I offered.

She glanced down at my leg, after curling her head sideways. "I believe you are on medication, right?"

"That doesn't mean I'm going to drink. But if I do, it's just wine. I'm doing it more for the environment instead of standing around here," I confessed.

She hesitated for a second but then gave in. "Okay! I was just going to pass by to see you for a few. But I guess we can do that. I don't have any plans," she confirmed.

Since it wasn't the leg I drive with that was injured, I wanted to drive us there. Besides, I wanted to feel like I was still active in some sort. The ride was long but smooth, through the farms, and finally at the vineyard. I bought a bottle of a white wine of her choice after we taste-tested a few samples. Then we sat at an outside table for some fresh air.

After washing down her throat with a few glasses of wine, Valerie decided to bring up what her dad had shared with her earlier today. How he caught us coming out of his office. "So what was so interesting about my dad's office? And why did you two have a suspicious look on your faces? That's what my dad remembers," she wondered.

I smelled my wine and took a light sip, followed by a smile. "Because of the pictures, I got the impression that you were daddy's little angel," I said.

"His only child," she interrupted.

"Yes, I'm aware, and because of the fact that I personally don't know many female artists, I was impressed by the sketch you did for him on that sheet," I confessed to her.

She did a small jump with her shoulders. "Thank you! That was at a dinner table with family. He was so happy that day," she recalled, and spoke further more about it. "I had just gotten done with my food and tried to capture that moment with a drawing," she added.

She brought me back to my curiosity of the picture that caught my eye. I was eager to bring that up. "There was one picture that I thought was beautiful," I mentioned.

She tilted her head, wondering which one. "What picture are you talking about?”

"You're not smiling in it but the angle and all was cute in my eyes. It's the one where you are wearing a green dress, with tan shoes. You are sitting and—”

She abruptly cuts me off in an angry fashion. "Yeah, I know! I know which one you're talking about!" Then she looked away from me.

What just happened? I asked myself. I was hoping I didn't ruin our date. So I tried to see what was the matter here. "I'm sorry, did I do something wrong?" I comforted.

Valerie looked back at me, and appeared to be trying to cool herself down. Then started to tell me about her mother. "I saw my mom that day, I hadn't seen her in a while. We had gotten into an argument before that picture was taken,” she revealed to me.

Assuming she didn't grow up with her mother, I tried to find out if I was right. "Was she not around when you were a child?" I asked.

"I lived with her half my life pretty much. Even when she left my dad for some scumbag womanizer, I still lived with her!" she yelled. I put my hand on top of her hand and lowered my head as she continued. "My dad was nothing but good to her. He suffered in silence and always told me he will never leave me behind.”

"And he's still there for you, Valerie," I added.

Her eyelids were slowly soaking up with tears. She told me some more about her mom's ex-boyfriend. "This man would play her, and play her! She would just forgive him… I didn't understand. I moved in with my dad at sixteen. She finally let him have me. I was relieved.” She sighed, while she shook her head, appearing to snap out of it. "I'm sorry, Sebastian, I don't mean to tell you all this. Maybe I had too much wine, I don't know,” she added.

I held her other hand and placed them together, as I slid a little closer to her face. "Hey, it's okay. We all have a story, no one's journey is full of glorious leaps with no bumps and scrapes,” I comforted.

She thanked me for the support, but then her mood changed a bit. She pulled her hands away, and an aura of seriousness came over her body. "Have you ever played with a woman's heart?" Her eyes were glued to my face.

"No!" I answered aggressively. "Not at all," I said.

"Well, let me ask you this. Have you ever beat on a woman?" she questioned.

I rolled my eyes, offended by this horrible question. "Listen, Valerie, I know better than that. I was raised to respect a woman. But I will tell you this. The day that I raise my fist at the woman I love, it's only because I'm showing her that her heart is in my hand. And I'm too afraid to lose it, so I'm holding her heart tight in my palm," I romantically described.

She smiled and didn't say a word for almost a whole minute. "I don't know about you, Sebastian. You're something else." She sighed. With a strong look of shame, she then added, "I hope you don't see me differently, me mentioning a bit of my past. What do you think of it anyways?"

I took away her cup of wine and sipped the last bit that was in her cup. My eyes came to a dead stop on her face, the whole time that the edge of the glass lay on my lip. "What do I think? I think I just slipped on your tears and fell in love with your story," I answered.

She rested her face on my hands briefly then jumped up in her seat and getting hit with a new idea. "Hey! Maybe when you're all healed up, you can visit one of my classes. You have a way with words. You might enjoy listening to my students, if it's okay with you," she offered.

"Yes, that would be interesting, my first time in a high school poetry class honestly," I admitted, while I was happy to be invited.

It was just an hour away from getting dark, we had spent a while at the vineyard, and it was time for us to leave. And me that I was a bit uncomfortable with this cast out in public.

The whole ride back to my place, she didn't say much but kept glancing at me, and I would look away with all smiles. We finally made it to my place.

"I can help you up the steps if you let me," she offered.

"I mean, it's only three steps to my porch, sweetie, but sure."

Her face lit up brighter than the moonlight over the seashore. I knew it wasn't because of the offer, but because of the simple word sweetie given at the right moment and the right place.

She walked me to my doorstep, in which I joked. "Damn. I almost feel less of a man. Isn't it supposed to be me at your door, making sure you get home safe after our date?" I flirted.

She laughed then pinched me while she rolled her eyes. "Sebastian,

I don't think there are any rules to that. Come on... But I did have a great time in your company," she admitted, then looked down our hand-holding. I knew she might just have been expecting a kiss.

But I didn't know that she was going to be the one to mention it. "Sebastian? What if our lips were to touch right now?" intimately, she asked.

I stood still with my crutches hugged under my armpits, as I stepped in close and leaned in an inch away from her face. "What if I told you the only the ones to get in between that would be our tongues?" I whispered to her.

We kissed for a what was probably just over one minute, but had the feel of an hour. The rhythm of both our bodies was that of a flow of peaceful water, with no patterns of waves.

She slightly pulled away to take one more joyful look at my face, and to caress my neck before we both said our good nights. I then went happily into the house. I sat down on the sofa, satisfied with my night. I felt as if I was sitting on a happy cloud that nothing could disturb me from. Until all of a sudden, I heard knocking that shook my door and rattled it like a snake. I jump out of my seat, stepping with my crutches fast up to the door. I wondered if was Valerie in a panic, only to realize it was Mike. I stared at him disturbed, through the glass, before I opened the door. When he rushed in, he almost tripped over my foot, even though I slid fast out of his way.

"Bro! What's wrong with you? You look like you want to puke your lungs out," I aggressively asked.

He stood momentarily pondering, with his clothes wrinkled as he observed me sitting calmly and awaiting an answer.

He exhaled in relief and took a seat next to me. "I went on a date with Lisa..." he simply replied.

I opened my arms with my palms up. "And??" I added. He clapped his hands once and raised his voice. "Well! I slept with her, there you go," he said abruptly.

I scratched my head with a little confusion. "That's what you wanted, didn't you? Um...congratulations?" I reacted to him. Mike has a heart at times, but for a night in bed with a girl, he's always shown me carelessness. What must have happened? I wondered.

"Yeah, man, I know. But shoot...it was more than that," he said, with his nose to his lap. I sat back and gave him his space to explain himself. "We went out, we ate, we had a good time!" The excitement in his voice quickly lowered. "We had sex, and it was good. But then she crawled to the corner of the bed and started crying her eyes out," Mike added, then sat his chin on his fist just like the thinking statue.

My curiosity was spinning circles inside my head at a fast pace. "And how come?"

"I don't know, Sebastian. She started to describe how her hus-band is a good man. And how she doesn't know why she's in bed with me. She stormed out of there disgusted, wanting to go home," he recalled.

Although Mike would support and help me through anything, he couldn't help his urge to enjoy a woman's sexual parts at all cost. So it was quite satisfying to see him show feelings of remorse. I enjoyed watching him feel sorry, ashamed, and guilty.

But after a few minutes, I still tried to support him. "Hey, Mike, it's cool. We need the use of mistakes, to better explain our positive actions in the future," I explained.

Becoming more relaxed, he simply agreed, but I then wondered. "Wait? I thought you've been with a married woman before, right?"

"Yeah, but the marriage was going down the drain, or the guy was an asshole. I just felt wrong, that's all" he confessed then contin-ued. "And I have to tell you, all the stuff you've been saying makes sense." He sighed, nodding while he played with his fingers.

Some of us learn life lessons faster than others, while some don't learn a thing at all. I just hoped that Mike took something positive out of his experience.

Suddenly out of the silence he turned toward me. "So what hap-pened? Did you hang out with your friend there, Valerie?" quickly he asked.

And I was excited to inform him. "Yes! Yes, I did," I answered with a glow in my eyes. "We had some wine, had great conversations. The talk even got emotional somewhere in between, and now I'm here home relaxing," I detailed.

As he daydreamed about what I said, he broke his focus, smirked. Looking happy for me. "Stay with her, man," he suggested. "I feel like she's for you. Hope it all works out." He wished me luck. Then off he went to walk back up to his part of the house.

I interrupted his steps and shouted just enough for him to hear me. "Hey, Mike? I know you can be a little crazy sometimes. But you still like a brother to me. I'm there when you need me," I assured him.

Barely looking over his shoulder, he simply replied, "Same here, bro.

Chapter 9

Magic in Her Kitchen

When I compliment your beauty, you don't have to thank me for what is already yours.

Valerie had invited me to her house for a tour, and to use my opinion on parts of it that could be fixed or changed a bit. But most importantly, to enjoy a home-cooked meal with her. As I arrived I could see how she took good care of her home. Grass was evenly cut, cinnamon color siding with silver roof shingles, that all together appeared to be pretty new.

The door was halfway opened, but the screen door was shut, as she had been expecting my arrival. I knocked on the screen door, and almost immediately I heard her feet walking in my direction. As she opened the door completely and reached for the handle on the screen, her smile and the white of her eyes shone as much as her fully exposed teeth. She stood her delicious frame in front of me. In black sandals with a small one-piece blue dress that hugged her body tight, which displayed her natural curves. Her dark hair in a bun with a touch of lip gloss on her lips. "Well, you're looking amazing," I com-mented as my eyes scanned her full body.

"I look okay, but thank you," she replied.

I slowly shook my head no, before taking a closer step with my crutches.

"You're welcome. But please, you don't have to thank me for your beauty," I whispered, while I breathed lightly on her lips. She caressed my neck briefly, followed by a tap kiss then walked me in. She had taken a whiff of my cologne, I noticed, and with her back turned she reacted. "Mmm…you smell yummy today," she mur-mured. I thanked her as we continued. "The food is done but let me show you around a bit."

She showed me the whole house then brought me to the bath-room to show me the sink vanity and how she wanted to replace it.

It looked like an old style to her, but it looked good to me. "I'll see what we can do once I'm good to go," I assured her.

We went down to her kitchen, where the air was filled with aro-mas of lemon salmon and cooked veggies. "Take a seat, honey," she offered, pointing at her dinner table with her back to me while she went to bring me my food.

I was taken aback when she called me honey, but at the same time my vision indulged the fine beauty of a woman she was. She called me honey, and I was still trying to figure out what kind of queen bee could ever make a honey like her.

"The veggies are still burning hot, be careful," she warned, as she sat my plate right under my nose, along with some white wine.

We ate in peace but occasionally smiled at each other. Once we both were done, she had squinted her eyes at me, tapped her lips with her fork. "I have a question." Then she got up and walked off with the empty plates. Turning my head toward her, I paused wait-ing for her question. She calmly sat next to me, while my curiosity was focused on what was I going to be interviewed about this time around.

"What is your question, sweetie?" I softly asked.

"Why are you single?"

I laughed, rolling my eyes to the ceiling. "Hey, explain this one thing to me, Valerie. Have you ever heard of a king crowning any woman just because his castle is empty?" I questioned.

Her head shook no in slow motion; she didn't even blink. "You are right. I get it." She sighed.

"I mean, Valerie, come on. There's no other way to answer such a question," I, annoyed, added then gazed at her as if something was off with her. "But the second I saw you, I knew you had to be single, you just had to be!" I blurted, as if I were implying that she had serious defects.

Her eyebrows went narrow, and she smacked my shoulder faster than killing a mosquito. "Hey! What is that supposed to mean?" upset, she asked.

I caressed the top of her hand and lowered my voice. "It's supposed to mean that by the time I walked into your life, that space was supposed to be available," I answered with seduction flowing in my voice.

She caressed my thigh and explained to me about her last relationship. "This is different for me. Because my last relationship he didn't say or do much that was passionate or romantic," she confessed.

I took her hand off my thigh, turned it around, and kissed her wrist while having my eyes glued to her face. "Whatever he did landed me right here with you. So I'm not even mad at him," I joked. We then enjoyed a good laugh to the thought of that.

She stared at my lips, which, as they went frozen, I stared at hers while she bit down on them. We kissed, savoring every bit of our mouths. She snuck her fingers under my shirt and gently slid them up to my chest. I kissed her breast while I pulled her body to mine by her ribs. When she kicked off her sandals, I spoke softly into her ear: "I just want to devour your body right now." I sighed.

While breathing on my mouth, she whispered back, "I'm not stopping you."

I looked over at the kitchen countertop, where there was a lot of space. And the coffee maker on the side. Softly I bit her neck, and with my injured leg shaking I walked her toward the counter.

She stopped me in my path, she asked, "What are you doing?" "Sitting you close to the coffee maker. That way, every morning while you are making breakfast, you think of us," I explained. After I had her on the countertop, I lowered myself just to shove my tongue in her belly button. we had sex there for a moment but ended up in every space of the kitchen. We then took it to her bedroom, my hands and tongue navigating all over her flesh while I was inside her. The air was filled with the musical sounds of my warm breathing and the bass of her moans. My skin became the playground to her sweat and the other way around. This climax had climbed to the max of explosion. We both had the look of wanting to cry, in response to how much we enjoyed our orgasms. We were both in a love trance, sexing each other until the point of falling asleep.

She woke me up in the morning. As she kissed my neck, she was already dressed to head to work. "How did you sleep?" she asked.

"I slept good, of course. But sorry, I know you have work. I'll get dressed right now," I promised her.

"I'm not rushing you," she said.

I hurried to the bathroom anyways to clean up a bit and brush with an unused toothbrush she had. My leg was hurting me just a bit, so I knew I needed my medications. I stepped my crutches fast into the kitchen, where I interrupted her pouring me coffee into a disposable cup.

We both took a glance at her countertop and smiled. "Sebastian, how many sugars do you want?"

"No…I'll take it just like that," I answered. The bitter taste of pure coffee was a craving I sometimes enjoyed. Besides, having to taste the sweetness of her body the whole night, why would I need any more sugar?

I took my cup along with her car keys to give her a head start while I turned mine on, also had hers running as well. I didn't feel I was done with trying to get her to think of me. Recalling her satisfy-ing reaction to my fragrance, my cologne caught my eye. Since I had it lying around on my passenger seat, the idea of giving her my scent crossed my mind suddenly.

I turned my head to the sound of her car door as it opened. She sat down faster than I could notice. I stepped out for one last kiss before I took off, with my cologne in hand of course. Soon as she rolled her window down, my face was all over hers, flooding it with kisses. "Listen, Valerie, if I'm not mistaken you are right-handed I believe?" suspiciously I asked.

She glanced at her right arm. "Yes, and why do you ask?"

I opened my hand and ask for her to place her right hand on my palm. Turning her hand, I sprayed a nice, wet load of my cologne on her wrist.

"What are you doing!" she shouted.

I calmed her down with my soft tone. "Shh…I'm only giving you my scent. So that you think of me every time you play with your hair, touch your face, or bite your pen while you are thinking," I disclosed.

So as her day went by and I wasn't there with her to enjoy her company, what I just did would let her know later. That even though I might not be there in body, I would sure be there in thought, bringing her back to her experience with me when in my presence. Recapping the moments in which we touched, we kissed, we sexed, and even us making love to our ears when we spoke to each other. To make her happy was first and foremost. But having her miss me was just one of the ways to keep her feelings for me alive. And even though I'd pay whatever price to buy her attention, I still wanted to be the man who stole her heart.

CHAPTER 10

Going through Therapy

Want to know why I never watched my step when I walked into your life?
Because I had no fear falling for you.

Some time had gone by, my cast was off, and I was on to go to ther-apy. I just started learning how to use the cane; I felt worse than a baby taking his first steps. With the cast off, every step I took my leg would shiver, my muscles would ache, and my emotions would con-tinue to hurt after I would compare both legs and notice how much weight my injured leg had lost.

"Sebastian, stop it!" demanded Valerie.

"What am I doing?" confused, I asked.

"You're stressing something that is going to be temporary. Look at it as a season. It's going to pass," she advised me.

I crumpled my face angrily and shoved my sight in her face. "Well, in that case then I feel like I'm stuck in winter!" I shouted.

She rubbed my back and laid her head on my shoulder. I stared at the top of her head and her dark hair, still mesmerized that she was here with me. I sighed and kissed the top of her head as I smelled the aroma of her clean hair. The warmth of her hand on my back, I felt that warmth to my lungs and almost to my chest. We sat in the lobby and waited for my appointment to my session. When we started, I did all types of resistant exercises and worked on balance. Isolating the movements to my recovering leg, I felt off-balance of course.

The therapist seamed tough on me. Or maybe that was just the light in which I was seeing it under. After we were done, I felt like a high school kid who had gotten beat up in a fight after school and was on his way home in defeat. I sat in Valerie's car, silent. Dazed, I stared out the window.

"How do you feel?" she asked.

"Like my leg was tied to a horse as he runs off in the forest," I replied.

She was quick to laugh and push me by my shoulder. "You're going to be fine. I mean your eyes did get moist and your face all red during therapy. I almost thought I would witness a tear rolling down," she teased.

"You're out of luck, sweetheart, because I don't do that crying crab," I added.

"Yeah yeah yeah, so big and macho, huh?" she responded, then puffed her chest out in an attempt to mock me.

I put my hands up and surrendered to her comment, then caressed her hand while she drove with the other.

As we come to a stop at a light, she turned toward me curiously. "Speaking about crying…have you ever cried over a woman?" she softly asked.

By this I sensed she was digging to see if I had any emotions. "Yes, I do have feelings, just so you know," I sarcastically answered.

She took a pause as if waiting for more. Her eyes were then open wide. "I take that as a yes??" curiously, she assumed.

"Yes," I said.

"Why is it that sometimes you make it harder to answer simple questions, honey?" she asked, frustrated.

I didn't want the discussion to turn difficult. It seemed for a second that that was where it was headed. An apology might just mellow things out, I assumed. "I'm sorry, Valerie, I'll try to change that a bit," I comforted her.

She brushed it off as if not a big deal then continued driving. In the attempt to make her feel better, I started to preach a few words. "I will say this about tears and hurting: if I was to hurt you, it should be the hurt of missing me all day. If I should ever make you cry, those tears will only be from joy. And my only anger toward you would only be about you not letting me know you arrived home safe from work." I then kissed and nibbled on the side of one of her fingers.

She put on a kitten face and hummed to herself. "Aww, Sebastian," she murmured, then kissed my hand right back.

"Why would I not want to keep you happy? I love the fact that you are here with me and my situation, and you don't have to be. I get nothing out of playing games with you, hurting you. I rather have your jet-black hairs on my bed than your crystal-clear tears on my floors," I promised her, while softly running the tips of my fingers across her cheek.

Her face and skin suddenly turned to a light shade of red. Her hand was warmer than fresh hotcakes, as she bit down on her lips. I knew I had her feeling more erotic moment to moment.

"Mm… I could listen to you talk to me like this all day." She sighed.

After an intimate ride home, I got myself settled in, sat on my sofa, then worked on some stretching taught to me by the therapist. With my leg straight, I hooked a towel on my bottom foot, right under my toes. Pulling to stretch out all that tensed area.

I could hear the birds outside my living room window. The soft breeze of my fan across the skin of my arms and leg. But no sweet smell of Valerie being next to me, no pleasing tone of her silky voice. I had shaken my head, confirming to myself that I was missing her around me already. The only fact that would bring me so much com-fort was to know that she felt the same about me while I wasn't there to touch and hold her. She was funny, artistic, and a poetry teacher! What more could I ask for? When she questioned me, or expressed her opinion on subjects or even on me, she would wonder where I would get my replies from. Did I write or read the things I'd say, or did I get the romantic things I do for her somewhere else? My answer to this would always be that when you have someone in front of you that could inspire these feelings, you don't need to read or buy your ideas anywhere else. The inspiration is right in front of you.

Even though I was home, I still wanted to take the time to do the things that would let her know that she still crossed my mind while she was not present. It's okay to say you think of someone, but it speaks volumes when the proof exists. I had a few "Caution, Wet Floor" signs in my garage. Using one of them, I took some burgundy paint out. With the tip of a small angled paintbrush, I wrote these words on the caution sign: "The reason I never watched my step when I walked into your life is because I wasn't afraid to fall for you."

I planned on placing the sign in front of her doorstep, so it would be the first thing she'd see once she got home. Mike and I had analyzed the sign as I had asked him for his opinion before I attempted the act.

"Can you make me one, Sebastian? I need that. I'll make use of it, trust me."

"You think it's a good idea, bro? Is that what you're saying?" I simply asked.

"Of course! Do it, man, I still need one, or I'll just use the phrase," he claimed.

The next morning, after she had left to start her day at work, I placed the sign at her doorstep. I couldn't wait to see her face, or even hear her voice on the phone reacting to the idea. I was at another therapy session waiting to start my appointment, this time without the comfort of her delicious company.

She called but with the speed of how I picked up, the line must have dropped. I heard silence, no answer, and eventually a click. Calling back, I could not get through; I had to hold myself back to let her call get through to me eventually.

"Sebastian!" she shouted. "Did you have me on hold?"

"Um…no, I'm at therapy."

"You sure? I felt like you did," she said.

This type of small confusion has happened to everyone. Instead of going back and forth like most people do, I wanted to close it off by making her smile to my correction of the dropped call. "Valerie, I will always be the answer to your calls. And trust me when I tell you, it's only in my arms where I would ever keep you on hold," I flirted.

After a quick yelp and giggle, she suggested. "You might as well start calling me Juliet one of these days. I feel I have my own personal Romeo with you." She chuckled.

I knew that by this time she had to have come across the sign I left at her door. I believe this call had everything to do with the finding of it. So I indirectly asked, "Hmm…I'm missing one of my caution signs. I wonder where I might have left it. You wouldn't hap-pen to know anything about that, do you?"

Again she giggled. "Gee, that's a good question. I did see something at my doorstep, but there's no wet paint or anything around to have such a sign placed there," she said sarcastically.

I myself laughed as well but under my breath.

"That was cute. I wasn't expecting that. If one of my neighbors saw me laughing and talking to myself outside my door, they would probably think I'm crazy. Thank you for that!" she shouted excitedly. Wishing I was there to see her reaction, I could only play the movie in my mind using her description of it from her point of view. And for her to appear to be insane to others was something I wanted to convince her not to view under a negative light. "Looking crazy to your neighbors, huh? If my doctor diagnosed me as being crazy over you, I would let him take the measurements of my torso, because I would need that straitjacket to be my size," I joked.

I heard the fast wind of her long inhalation.

"Do you have space for me today, Sebastian?"

"Of course I do," I simply answered.

"I just want to give you a hug," she mumbled.

"You call it hugging, sweetie, I call it holding. Me holding on to who matters to me most," I confessed.

She rushed off the phone to speed up our date with each other. "Bye, honey, I want to hear how your therapy went today in person. We can take a walk if you'd like, I know you need it," she suggested.

We agreed on taking a peaceful journey through the local park. The exercise was meant for my leg, but this precious time was meant for each other. And we slowly paced through the park, stepping in the same rhythm together, along with the use of my cane.

It was the middle of October, and the fall leaves flooded the floors with its beautiful display of nature. I had a thin silver hoodie, sky-blue jeans, and casual cement-gray sneakers. Valerie was still in her teacher attire, an all-black suit with blazer, and a cherry-red scarf with black-and-white lines.

"You look comfy today," she said, while she observed my every step

"I am, and I'm feeling stronger as well," I confirmed.

She turned her face to me with wide eyes and responded in a high-pitched voice, "That's good!"

I then mentioned her clothes and how I might look walking next to her. "I almost feel that I'm one of your students, and you're walking me while giving me a pep talk," I added.

"Oh okay. On that note, I know that you are older than me. But you never know! You might learn a thing or two from me this young gal," she said, while she brushed her shoulder, teasing me.

My eyes traveled up and down her body while I tasted my lips. "Mm…well, I am willing to go for my bachelor's in the study of your body. Pleasing you is what I want to major in. Just to show you that this student can and will impress his teacher." Seductively I flirted with her while I rubbed on her.

She almost rubbed her breast to the thought of it. "Oh god I would love that! But this is the wrong place," she added, then slith-ered her fingers down my palm and between my fingers.

Holding hands, we walked in peace, smiling down at our steps. I wanted to hear more about her day at school, to show that I had interest in her loving job. "So was there anything interesting that occurred in your day at school earlier?" I asked with an open ear.

She lit up faster than a switch does a bulb. "Of course! Every day is interesting. Yesterday I exhausted my students with fast-paced free writing. Today I had them do exercises on homophones and ambiguity," she described.

It was as if I were in class with her the way she would detail it all. Continuing the conversation, I added, "You must love the feeling of knowing that these kids learned this, especially through you."

"It's more than that. Poetry is a good tool to build skills that they will need in the future," she said.

I then asked for her to describe some. "Aside from helping them think creatively, it builds conversational skills, helps convey feel-ings, and you can't forget about how it improves storytelling!" she answered delightedly.

There is never a time that Valerie speaks dull about her teach-ings. Every word she speaks about the subject carries much weight of passion. I was happy to give her the credit she deserved. "I know you are great at what you love to do. The principal should feel lucky to have a teacher such as yourself within his staff. And if he doesn't, just tell me! So I can kick his ass," I joked.

The burst of her laughter made me skip a step in my stroll. "You won't do that, come on. And if there is anyone that I would wish that would never to take me for granted, that man would be you," she murmured, with her head low and her eyes slowly coming up to my face.

We had come to a sudden stop. She turned her body toward me. Her eyes locked on mine with a face softer than baby skin, and a look as serious as those in a funeral.

With all the emotions inside me, I tried to match that same stillness and seriousness. Meaning everything I was just about to express to her. "Valerie. I know what I have, and I know who I am. To have you then lose you, just to realize what I had? No... But if I lose anything, let me lose myself in your eyes. But please don't show me the way out," I expressed with passion.

Her nose was just a hair from touching mine, and my lips could feel her breathing, and she would take back-and-forth glances at my eyes and cheekbones. "You're something else, Sebastian... Where has a guy like you been all my life?" she softly asked.

I wasn't sure if she was being sarcastic. As it had sounded like those words were easily falling out of her mouth, with no passion behind it. But when I answered I did so with all honesty. "Where was I this whole time? I'm not sure, maybe life was preparing me for a special woman like you," I answered.

She then slid her thumb back and forth on my bottom lip. "It's possible," she added.

I placed my hands on the side of her neck, and in slow motion I pressed my lips upon hers. Most people take a plane to paradise. I took a plain kiss of Valerie's lips that sent both of us to paradise. In that moment, nothing else mattered, with our eyes closed and our tongues dancing in our mouths. To me as well as her, the rest of the world didn't exist. It was just us.

We heard the tapping of two pairs of shoes walking together, coming close. Our moment was broken by a couple who laughed under their breath to the sight of us kissing.

"How's your leg feel so far?" she asked, as we started to walk again.

"It feels a little stiff but not bad at all. Thank you for asking, honey." I sighed.

She hugged my arm and kissed my sleeve. "You make me want to take care of you. It's sad to see your demeanor change all of a sud-den," she comforted.

I slowed my pace by a lot. "What do you mean by that?" I questioned.

"You see, when I first met you, you had more life to your whole aura. And don't get me wrong! I understand. It just touches me a bit to notice the change," she detailed.

I had no words for her observation of me. It bothered me for a moment as flashes of me dropping to the ground. Back at that basement came tumbling down my memory of the whole event.

I tried to laugh it off quickly. "I'm okay, really. I'll be back to normal like you told me before," I mumbled while I stared down at my leg.

"Yes, you will. Oh wait. Hold still," she demanded, then reached to my shoulder, as my eyes followed her hand. I expected an insect of some sort to be removed off my hoodie. But it was just a loose string from the fabric.

"Yeah, it's just a string. You jumped as if you were expecting a spider or something," she teased.

As she went to throw it out, I grabbed her hand quickly and gripped her fingers. "Wait a minute! Don't throw this away. I need it!" I demanded.

She leaned her face away like a cobra does and looked me up and down, confused. "What the hell do you need a piece of string for?" she asked, annoyed.

"Maybe I can tie this string to a needle and sow your heart back together from all its past breakage," I whispered.

"Oh god! Sebastian, are you going to stop?" she bickered.

"Listen, woman. One day you're going to miss me talking sweet to you if I were to no longer do so," I predicted.

She nodded, raising one shoulder. "You are right, I probably will," she added.

I saw her pondering. I was wondering what might be develop-ing in her mind at that point. But before I could even ask, she beat me to it.

"So how does this work? Do you play with words in your mind's eye before you say them?" she asked.

I tapped my cane with my thumb while walking, as I tried to think on how was going to put this, so she'd easily understand. "You ever notice how an opportunist sees a come-up in every obstacle?"

"Yes," she said.

"And how a regular person sees a job as just a worthless job? But an entrepreneur sees a stepping stone?" She nodded once again.

"Well, from all the hurt and sadness in the world, I choose to see the beauty in the simple things that exist in our lives," I answered, as I summed it all up.

"With the help of me, of course?"she interrupted.

I then stopped us again, raised her hand to my face, kissing every finger one by one before I curled her hand into a fist. Softly I bit the back of her hand, while having her eyes locked on my face the whole time. "Yes, Valerie, because of you," I confessed.

She wrapped her arms around me, resting her head on my shoulder in a sleeping fashion. Her lips cuddled on my hoodie. "Hold me, Sebastian... Just to feel you here with me is enough at this present moment," she softly expressed to me.

One fact that I knew for sure was that there was no dictionary printed anywhere in this world with the perfect word to describe how special this woman was to me. I was here to stay, not play. I didn't enter Valerie's life in search of an exit. More than wanting to say this, I was motivated to prove this as true.

Some men learn how to get into a woman's bed, how to seduce her enough to sleep with her. Although that is a skill, it's not the only skill when it comes to our precious women who walk our world with us. Boys will find a way to get in a woman's pants, but that's it. A boy cannot keep a woman because an ongoing relationship is a whole other skill only played by a man. A much important skill than the one a boy knows. Only a man knows how to sleep with, then keep, the woman he loves. And it's a skill that is constantly in the works during the whole relationship. A technique that all of us men should pursue as part of one of our life goals. And mine had just started.

CHAPTER 11

The Two of Us and the One Life We Share

After meeting with so many wrong turns and detours in the road of life, I was happy I found my destination with you.

After many dinners I had at Valerie's house, this time around we rested in the dark, inside her living room. I lay on her sofa with her on top. A hand on one part of my chest and her head on the other. With both our faces toward the only light in the room, which was coming from her fifty-gallon fish tank. Having pillow talk while observing the many different fishes. Swimming through and around her idea of fancy ornaments, she had spread out for them in her small aquarium. From the castle, treasure box, to the sunken ship. And her favorite, which was the starfish.

"What can be more relaxing than swimming freely, especially through the exotic world of the ocean?" she asked me softly.

"I would say flying," I answered.

"And I would say you are wrong," she teased.

"Now that I mentioned flying, how come you don't have the crashing plane in your collection?" I questioned with a grin as I teased her back.

"Because I think it's lame," she blurted.

I couldn't help but laugh in reaction. I could lay here all day with this woman and enjoy her sexy pillow talks as well as her jokes and sarcasms.

"I do see you have a lot of starfish ornaments. How come?" I questioned.

She pressed her index finger on both my lips, her eyes shining on my face like two light bulbs. "Don't you say anything about my starfishes," she warned.

"I have nothing bad to say about your starfishes. Only that you are my star… And I do not have to fish for that" I flirted.

She hovered over me with her face down over mine. And her jet-black hair covering the sides of my face like a bed-curtain canopy. "You're so sexy, I swear," she gushed, before she bit and kissed my lips.

We slowly stripped, almost completely naked, sliding our hands all over our bodies and licking every bit of our flesh that was exposed for the moment.

We came to a complete stoppage when she pulled away from me. "Wait!" she shouted, as she gasped for air. "Give me a minute, honey, I'll be right back," she promised, then sped out of the living room.

All I heard next was her bedroom door shut. I was left on the sofa hot and unsettled, with a volcano broiling within. I just wanted to explode, desiring the sex that I was used to with her, when out of nowhere without hearing her bedroom door open I heard the steps of her sexy walk. A walk that I had embedded in my memory since the beginning. Tapping her way to the living room from the hallway. I saw her step out from the dark, one foot of red pump shoes placed on the floor and the rest of her body followed.

She wore one of her apple-red blazers with a pearl-white tie that hung in between her exposed breasts. Completely naked underneath, with her delicious caramel, skin which I loved so much. Getting closer to my sitting body, I was slowly starting to smell that she was wearing Kiwi body spray. From my first inhalation of the aroma, my body's temperature rose. My skin moistened to a sensitive state.

She was just a foot away before she stopped in front of me. "You said you would study my body, right? Well, here I am, my love. Where on this teacher's body would you like to start?" she passion-ately asked.

I reached for my cane that I wasn't using anymore, but which lingered around and was within close reach. I hooked the handle part behind her lower back, grabbing her. I pulled her toward me. With the aggressive manner I pulled her in, she yelped and fell in a sitting position on my lap. With her breasts in front of my neck and me looking up at her.

"You look like a math teacher," I added, as she smiled back and waited for me to continue. "In that case… I want you to help me subtract your past, add me as the gift to your present, times our good times by many. But please, Valerie, let's never divide us," I seductively detailed.

She shoved her breasts in my face and caressed my scalp with her nails as I slid my fingers from her ribs to her lower back, and softly up the sides of her spine. Slowly traveling the tip of my tongue all in between her breast. Landing my mouth on her nipple to deliver a bite. Not hard enough to bleed but enough to get an "ouch" fol-lowed by a pleasing moan.

With her thumbs covering my ear canals and the rest of her fingers pressing against the back of my neck, she forced my face back up to hers as she reached down for a kiss. We were tangled like two snakes slithering all over each other's bodies. In my own imagination I could see the steam coming off us as we lusted over ourselves. I picked her up and placed her under me on the sofa. I pulled her loosened tie with my teeth and took the rest of her clothes off as she sneaked her hands into my jeans. With the same breathing as if in a sauna or steam room, she reached behind her head and pulled off one of the pillows that was in the way.

I grabbed the pillow from her before tossing it across the room, while I stared at the pillow I began to express: "I love the talks we have before and after sex. It's just healthy to have such a chemistry as we do. I must say that our pillow talks are just food for thought. But us making love…well, that's the vitamins and nutrients to your heart." I whispered all this to her.

She dug her nails into my muscular chest as she squirmed her body all underneath me. "Mmm…grab me, baby, I'm all yours," she gushed, as she surrendered her body to me.

I had to stop us at that moment to make sure I informed her of a special confession I had and could finally put it into words. "Valerie. You being spontaneous and creative to pull this sexy, naked-teacher idea all of a sudden is exactly what I'm referring to when I call you beautiful. It's your actions…and who you are that I find irresistible." I sighed.

We made love the whole night, and fell asleep to the soothing sounds of her fish tank's flowing water. The next morning while lying with her in the tub, both our bodies were bathing from almost our chest and down. As I sat in this soapy, fog-like water, she sat behind me with her breasts pressed on my back, her hands rubbing down my arms. This Olay Shea Butter Body Wash played like a lotion, as she massaged and washed down my body.

"Sebastian?" she mumbled.

"Yes, love?"

"Remember the deal we made about you visiting my class?" she asked.

"I wouldn't call that a deal, but I remember the idea."

She kissed the back of my head then asked if I could make it today after we get dressed.

"I'm not sure how I will do in front of a class. I don't even know what to say!" I stressed.

"Going once…going twice," she counted, provoking me to answer.

I turned around with my knees in between her legs. Grabbed her waist with my arms and slid her wet, naked body to my built structure shining from the soap. "Count no further, I'm sold," I assured her.

On our way to her school while she drove, we talked over some piano music. I was never used to this type of melody with no words. But she preached to me how it was relaxing and influenced creative thought and evoked emotions. Most of it was romantic or calming. I also made use of this calming music to relax me while she sped up, sporadically racing to her class.

But then I heard a tune that swooped out from the dark and grabbed my attention, faster than an owl steals a mouse off the ground. "Whoa what's this?" I asked.

"Don't tell me you like this?" she continued, surprised. "This is from a sad place in the musician's heart," she mentioned.

I looked around as if lost. "And?"

"What do you mean and?" she shouted. "You called the poem I gave to you at the hospital dark and depressing… This is no differ-ent," she debated.

And she was right, but I still thought this was a beautiful display of music. Sadness is not a pleasant feeling of course. But the power of art lies in the creative beauty, in which the artist can form from the emotions of even sadness.

"I know, but this is different. And keep your eyes on the road!" I warned, as she had gotten closer to the curb.

"I know how to drive, officer!" she said, as she teased my reaction.

I took a quick attempt at bouncing back from her sarcasm. "Yeah, I wonder what school of driving taught you how to drive me crazy over you. But it's working and you deserve a citation for that," I replied with a flirty smile.

She laughed then decided to put her own spin to continue our playful, romantic talk. "I don't know either. But since I met you, or should I say since our head-on collision with each other, I report this was no accident. This was destined to happen. More in the lane of being love driven," she flirted.

I opened my eyes in surprise and slowly turned my head toward her. "Damn, baby…tell me more. Now I'm the one saying that I could listen to you talk to me like this all day," I excitedly shouted.

Her smile stretched in full with the corners of her eyes match-ing the width. "I love you, Sebastian. And it takes a lot for me to say that," she mentioned with a sure look on her face, as if she were in court testifying.

Finally, at her place of work, we parked. She smirked at me in a daze then squeezed my hand. "It seems you care about my line of work, and I have to say I also brought you here so you can see what I go through and how important to me my classes are, as well as my students," she confessed.

"You guessed it right, baby. I care about your passion. Although we come from two separate worlds, two separate lives. I'm happy to share one life with you, separate from the rest of the world," I declared.

"I'll be there for you as I was with your therapy. Remember that I live in your world too, Sebastian," she promised.

After this moment in the car, we then entered the high school where I was to witness her practice her teachings. In her room we were setting everything up for the class that was about to fill the room soon. Students started to walk in as we awaited all in atten-dance. One by one they would look at me as they walked in, with a face of curiosity. I haven't been in a high school in so long. Plus these young faces made me feel my thirty-five years of age even more.

When class started, she introduced me as her boyfriend. And the whole class sung "woo" as Valerie did a good acting job hiding that she wanted to blush. "I have him here today for impressing me with his words that carry much color and movement," she expressed. She stopped briefly to glance over at me and smile. "And also, because he won my attention with this quote right here: 'after meeting with so many wrong turns and detours in this road of life, I was happy to have found my destination with you.'" She sighed.

The class was in awe, with their faces to her. But giggles were also scattered across the room between the students.

"All right, people," began Valerie. "Yesterday I had all of you pick a poem from any poet to read out loud. And express what it meant to you and why did this grab your attention," she said to the class, while she pointed her pen at the crowd as she paced side to side. "By now most of you are having your ways of expressing your-selves. And I'm impressed at the improvements of the class as a whole itself." At this point she leaned her butt against the front of her desk and crossed her arms and faced all of them. "To start this class off, I would like for you all to take turns describing to me. What is it that poetry means to you? How does it feel? What have you learned or come to realize? You can be very expressive or simple. This is just to start us off today," she requested from the students.

I looked around as one by one they raised their hands and took turns to speak. I was impressed by most of them and how they spoke. This showed me how good of a teacher Valerie was. And how focused and attentive she had become toward her goals with the students. I turned my attention to her, and she looked even sexier to me doing what she loved to do. It was like a light shining over her. As I blocked off the background and focused on her beauty, I was devouring the very sight of her. With my vision starving for such an image as her-self. Some people in our lives can be out of this world to us. And to me she was my planet Venus; my eyes would always orbit her body.

As the class came to an end, I took notice of a shy young man. Matching the description of one of Valerie's favorite students, I recall her telling me about him. After the bell rung and the students were leaving the room, she signaled for the shy kid to stay. She wanted to speak with him. Now that the classroom was empty, Valerie turned to me.

"Honey, this is William I was telling you about," she introduced.

"How are you, William?" I greeted as I shook his hand. "I read some of your stuff," I mentioned. I took a quick glance at Valerie as she opened her eyes wide, warning me with her sight to say some-thing nice. "I, I think it's very deep. You come from a strong place with your material," I stuttered.

He wandered his eyes on the ground. "Thank you…" he barely mumbled.

He was dressed in dark colors and was holding his head down, and I could tell that William wasn't much of the social type. Valerie soon enough thanked him and excused us, letting him proceed to his next class.

"So that was William I see."

"Yes, don't mind him, he's a very shy kid. A good student…and very respectful," she added.

"No worries," I blurted, brushing it off. As the room was empty at the moment, I grabbed her hand and pulled her into my clutches. Hugged, kissed, then smelled her neck.

"What are you smelling?" she asked, giggling.

"You smell like tonight's dinner, the only meal on my menu," I whispered sexually to her.

"I'd rather have you at any time of day," she replied while she tasted her lips.

I rolled my eyes and pulled away. "Jesus, Valerie! There's enough of me for all four of you, so don't be greedy!" I shouted.

She gazed at me with the eyes and eyebrows of an owl. "What the hell did you just say?" she yelled as if wanting to kill me.

"I'm talking about the morning you, the afternoon you, the evening you. And let's not forget, the 'looking so good in bed sleep-ing' you. That's all four of them. Who did you think I was talking about??" I teased.

"Whatever, baby," she mumbled while blushing then pushed me off her.

The day came to a pleasant close later that night. I was up early with Mike at the store, to go over a list of different types of wooden door trims we had to pick up.

"Does your leg feel any different?" wondered Mike.

"I get pain at night sometimes, but not so much like before."

"Oh…okay. Hold on, bro," said Mike, as we stopped to reach for another cut of trim. And me checking off numbers from the list.

"I tell you this, though. Before I even reach down to my leg, Valerie is already digging her fingers exactly where I'm tensed at. And massaging softly where it hurts," I described to Mike.

He looked down slowly, pushing the cart forward. "You're a different type of happy, my friend, like a new man. Stay that way, bro," he suggested, appreciating the new me and not missing who I was.

"I appreciate that, Mike. Now I can have all my new memories of fun with just one woman, instead of scattered stories with differ-ent girls," I described while I smiled and nodded.

"Hey, that's cool and all, honestly. But I don't regret any from back then," he assured me.

"Well, I don't either really. I—"

He interrupted me as he completely cut me off. "But yo! Bro, I've gotten stronger! hurry up and come back to the gym so I can whoop that ass!" shouted Mike in a taunting manner.

"Oh don't you worry! You know who reigns supreme in that world!" I shouted back at him. "Oh, Mike, speaking of the gym. I have to pick up Valerie later at her gym. She just started going again," I informed him.

He started rubbing his chin with his eyes up, thinking.

"What's the matter?" I asked.

"Just thinking of how much to pay the kid I got helping me," he added.

"Don't overpay him, though, if he's not making up to the hard work. But for now, let's pay for this stuff and get it to the house," I suggested.

After running errands with Mike, I decided to stop at the flower shop to surprise Valerie with the random gesture. A dozen mixed roses, six reds and six whites. And a postcard that I wrote on, that read, "While our happiness was happening, you once asked me what is it that makes me happily ever after? And today I answer you—that it's me being happily always after you that makes me happily ever after."

I sped up, hoping to catch her right when she was about done with her session. I was parked for ten minutes, and watched each person that walked out the gym, hoping to see her. Suddenly I saw that seductive walk of hers, the way she would sways while she walked. She had on a raspberry top and black spandex gym pants and a water bottle at hand. I stepped out of my truck with the flowers behind me. She had a smile wide enough to wrap around her head.

"Baby!" she shouted excitedly while she approached closely. She opened her arms wide, and I snatched her water bottle off her grip and pulled back from hugging her. She froze and looked at me, shocked.

"I'm going to need this," I demanded, as I took a swig of her water. "Oh perfect, it's room temperature water," I added. I then swung around the flowers right in between us and started pouring the rest of the water into the flower vessel.

She blushed then put both hands over her mouth. "Thank you!" she gushed.

We kissed briefly, even with the flowers in the way. The soft rose petals rubbed on our necks as we seemed to block them out and enjoy our kisses like a dessert after a good meal.

"Oh wait!" She stopped me, as she started to rub one of her eyes. "I think I got something in my eye, maybe from the flowers," she guessed.

I caressed her hand and claimed that she was making this up. "Honey, please, don't use that excuse just so you can blink in my direction," I flirted, as she continued to blush.

"Stop it, Sebastian, I really did have something in my eye," she confessed.

I started to laugh, loving every second of her presence. Valerie slapped my chest once. "If I wanted to blink, smile, or stick my tongue out at you I would just do it, baby," she teased, fol-lowed by a pinch of her fingers on the sides of my stomach.

"I would never blink at you, Valerie. Only because I want both of my eyes enjoying your every presence in full body," I seductively whispered, while my eyesight slid across her soft lips. I took her hand and guided her to dig deeper, into the flowers to feel the postcard that was tucked in.

"Postcard?" she questioned.

"Read it, my love," I demanded.

As her eyes traveled across the card, reading it completely, she had a face of wanting to cry but she didn't. "Sebastian, what's the idea for?" she wondered.

"Nothing," I answered. "Today is no special day, it's just that I wanted to surprise my honey," I confessed.

I looked around and noticed too many people paying attention to us. So I led Valerie to the passenger side, opened the door, and sat her down. We could continue our chatter in the truck for the moment.

"I missed you today, baby. I kept thinking about you while I was exercising," she murmured while massaging my hand.

I picked up her chin with my index finger and adjusted her face to mine. "How can you miss a man that has never left your thoughts? In a way, I was inside of you this whole time," I passionately replied.

She rubbed her hand on my inner thigh, brought it up close to my zipper. "I would have you right here if it were appropriate," she declared.

Even though fall was at its end, it was a very warm day out for this time a year. In the meantime, before winter comes, we have to enjoy these pleasant outside temperatures. It was just about to rain, and I also was informed earlier that her dad was going to close his computer store early for some unknown reason. Thinking of how flat and secluded his rooftop was, I was hit with a delicious idea.

"Do you have keys to your dad's store?" I asked impatiently. "There at my house, but yes," she answered. "Um…why? What are you thinking?"

"I'm not done surprising you," I answered with confidence. On my way to the house, I randomly stopped and rushed in and out of a store for two transparent raincoats. Then we made it to her house, and she opened the passenger door.

"I should go change," she suggested.

"Trust me, you won't need to. Just get the keys," I promised her. When we arrived at the store, after she shut the alarm off, we headed toward the latter to go up to the roof. I know that in her dad's office there was the umbrella she used when I first met her that one rainy day. I snatched it and shoved it in my raincoat.

"What are you doing?" she asked with a smile.

"We might need this too. Take off your clothes, baby, and put the raincoat on," I demanded.

I assisted her while I ripped my clothes off as well. Standing right by the latter before we went up, I kissed her one more time and hugged her. "Listen, Valerie. There's never a right time to do any-thing, even personal goals. But aside from that, the best moments in our lives happen just like this. Unpredictable, spontaneous," I said.

She chuckled and poked her a finger on my chest. "And you, mister, are always saying you're not one for surprises," she recalled, while pressing her torso on mine.

She was right, and one day I'd rephrase that. I grabbed her by her hand, setting my sights all over her. "I'll shower with you in the rain, before I ever shower myself in your tears," I said.

We headed up to the roof. As soon as I picked a safe spot to lie on, she placed her hands on my back. "Turn around," she asked of me. "And just sit down."

We kissed as the rain started to come down even harder. Both our raincoats were huge and served as a blanket at times. She sat on my lap as I was hard inside her, grinding me with my face shoved in her neck. We were getting a light massage by the rumble of raindrops all over our coats. Moaning in my ear, she squeaked, "Oh my god, Sebastian!" I felt the pleasure of her body showing me that she was more than satisfied and exploding inside from the orgasms. Even though on the ground, I remained in a sitting position. While I looked at her naked body through the clear coat, I kept getting even more excited. Her back would arch as she would briefly yell up to the rain, then put her face back down. Closing her legs on my waist, I would feel her thighs as they shivered in climax.

I spun her around, laid her body down, and pulled the umbrella out, shaking off the water that it already had. "While you're lying down, put the umbrella over your face. It's raining too hard right now," I instructed her.

She opened her legs and smiled, knowing my intentions. I put my hoodie over my head then shoved my face in between her thighs. Having a hard time holding the umbrella, she screamed and moaned. Digging her nails all over my scalp. I could tell at times she would try to silence herself. But her body being pleased by my tongue moving inside her did not let her at all. I wasn't worried if anyone heard us; they would have to guess where the noise was coming from.

Those were the things and ideas I was talking about when I tried to school Mike. When I try to explain to him that, it's not always what you say. Sometimes it's also what you do, because memories such as these don't cost much. But to the one you love it will remain in high value to their heart.

We spent a lot of time in the rooftop, but after a while of being drenched we got dressed and headed to her home. Lying in bed after a good shower, we cuddled in peace. She laid her head on my chest. And with the tips of her fingers sliding up and down my stomach, she stared down at my underwear.

"Sebastian?" she asked. "You had me on my kitchen counter, you had me on the store's rooftop. Is there another place you had in mind?" she wondered.

"I wish I could have you in a pool of strawberries. While you wear a bikini made of grapes, so I can eat my way down to your naked body before having sex. But that's impossible," I answered.

She bit her lips and moaned to the thought of it. "Mmm…you never know, anything that's imagined can one day be a reality," she whispered.

"Another thing," she added. "When I'm with you, it's so different."

I sat up just a little. "What do you mean?" I questioned. "It's just that. Making love with you feels more like we are in another realm, far away from anything. I have no way of explaining it," she expressed.

"I feel the same way, my love," I agreed.

She placed her palm on my palm, spreading out my fingers with hers. "Like we are one," she guessed.

I shook my head aggressively, in disagreement to that assump-tion. "I wouldn't say we are one. You know how many relationships have crumbled because one of the two thought it was all about one? One person, one idea, one opinion, and so on," I said.

She exhaled quickly. "I guess you're right if you see it like that, yes," she said, while still pondering the thought. "I mean our sex feels spiritual. Mind, body, and soul. That's what it's called, right?" she asked.

"It's just called making love, Valerie. It takes over our whole self, once magic is at play," I said, then smiled at her for expressing our sex in that manner. "And as for mind, body, and soul, please don't mind when my body makes love to your soul," I added.

She giggled. At this point she was already used to my consistent flirting.

"What am I going to do with you, Sebastian? You drive me crazy over you." She sighed.

I kissed the top of her head, on that sexy black shining hair of hers. "I'm going to the kitchen, if you want me to bring you any-thing," I offered.

"Yes, my water that's in the fridge. But before you do," she added, "I bought you a pair of blue sandals your size. They're under the bed."

Surprised she bought me this little gift, I began to observe the whole design. I could see why she bought them for me. On the heel it had the image of a nut screw as round as the ball of the heel. The toes also had nut screws ranging from big toe until little toe, and the strap was a socket wrench. A handyman's perfect gift if he needs some creative sandals around the house.

"I like it, but…why the color blue?" I asked, looking puzzled. She quickly sat up from bed. "What do you mean? That's your favorite color!" she shouted. Then she tried to help me recall, "The first day when we had breakfast, you told me your favorite color was blue."

I pretended to correct myself. When I helped her recall what I claimed, I actually said, "No, baby, I never said my favorite color was blue. What I said was that it blew my mind to know that my favorite woman was out enjoying breakfast with me," I teased.

Her eyes went narrow and her forehead wrinkled before hitting me in the head with a flying pillow. "You jerk! I thought I was going to have to go to the store and change them!" she shouted.

I enjoyed the brief laughter but then admitted, "Yes, baby, I did say it was blue. It's just that since you joke on me sometimes. I have to get you back," I confessed.

Laughing, she pulled the bedsheets from her breast and over her shoulders. "Go get my water!" she demanded, while still smiling and shaking her head in bed.

Even though this didn't count as being angry, I barely experi-enced her ever being mad at me. Not everything was meant to stay perfect, and disagreements may occur. But there was no need to rush these types of headaches either. And even when she can become upset, downcast, as long as we remained on set, side-by-side in our path together, then we both will be all set.

How I treated Valerie was nowhere near to the treatment I had toward Isabel. More than likely, Isabel would be in disbelief as to what kind of man I've become in a relationship. I lied to Valerie about my misbehavior in past relationships, and never wanted to speak much about my last one. I didn't see the reason to; it was all left behind me and should stay there. I felt much better to be out of that old skin of mine and walk a new path, as a new me and a special her.

What my past missed out on with me, now my future is blessed to see of me. I have something to look forward to with Valerie. By now we've been on countless dates, created countless romantic ideas, made love so many times in the right moments, and I also improved parts of her house—fixing and changing the interior out of my own pocket. Knowing we had a future together, this investment was nec-essary. Like high-value shares in a rich company, I felt a high to value and share in my life, the riches of her company. Who she was, what she meant to me, and what we could become together. All the things I've done by now and I was nowhere near finished with us.

CHAPTER 12

An Unwelcome Visit by the Haunting of My Past

The devil stomped on my heart, making wine from the blood, and was drinking to my broken story.

Coming close to a year of my accident in late spring also meant coming close to the day I met Valerie. Which was a better way to remember those times. I was running off track with my mind racing before she walked into my life. And although she won the Olympics with me by simply walking in, all she did now was run through my mind. I got these signals at times that reminded me of what I needed before I even needed it.

For instance, if I had a stomachache, I knew it had to be something I ate. If I was tired and exhausted, it was definitely because I didn't get enough sleep the previous night. That was why I didn't spend too much time away from the woman that made my body feel good, as soon as I laid my eyes on her. Because I started to feel off-balance, like something was missing. Why would I do such a thing to my well-being? To be with this woman meant taking it to the next level, I started to realize. I had never developed the feeling before to ever get engaged. But Valerie seemed to have aroused this desire in me.

Is it too early to ask? I wondered. While I was indulged with my tongue in her mouth right outside of her school. This was the way she was making me feel about us at this point. "Okay, baby, wait." She stopped me during our kissing. "I have to go back to class in a bit. Am I seeing you later?" she asked.

"Of course!" I shouted. "I'm so jealous of this coffee mug right now," I teased, as I poked the mug with my finger. "Because I made you the coffee, brought it to you, and now it's going upstairs. And you're sending me away?"

"Or is it because during class my mouth will be all over the mug and not on you?" she teased back.

I chuckled while I played with her hair. We then kissed one more time before I went on my way. I had paid her a visit on her break, and now I was walking from the front of her school to the parking lot. For some odd reason this walk felt as if it were being watched. The air was so still, and everything so quiet, I could almost hear the leaves on the top of the trees slightly moving. The grass was like a loud crunch after every step I took. What kind of surprise was ahead of my day? I questioned myself. Or was it just me feeling weird?

All of a sudden, in front of me, a familiar face walked in my direction—blond hair with a pretty face. We locked eyes for a moment, but her face had the look of a butcher when he looks at a chunk of meat while he has his meat cleaver in hand. As she walked right by me, thrusting her body and roughly swinging arms and legs, I heard her softly exhale in disgust. I looked back after I passed her, as she did the same. I shook my head, wondering what her issue was, but I then just got to my truck and just sat there. I stared in silence at the school, trying to recall who she was, as this seemed to have happened quick, and I might not have gotten a good look at her face. After a brief moment I brushed it off, turned the truck on, and decided to call Mike about work duties.

Then, all of a sudden, I saw the same woman walking out of the school minutes later, along with a student who appeared could be her little sister. As Mike's phone rung twice, I hung up and put my phone away, because it all came together to me all at once. The blonde, me calling Mike, this was one of the girls that was at the coffee shop with us a while back. That was Anna I saw! Lisa's friend. I had forgotten who she was not only because I had only seen her for a few minutes back at the coffee shop, but also, why would I want to remember some girl that I didn't want anything to do with? And even a better question, if I didn't do anything to her for her to feel animosity toward me, what was the disgusted look for? Was there something I was missing?

I noticed that she spotted me sitting in the truck, while they both walked to her car. Anna then pointed me out to the younger girl, as they both sat in the car and were conversing while they looked over at me. My phone started ringing; it was Mike calling back. I waved the back of my hand at Anna, moving my head and signaling with my lips with the word what? Like as if I were asking what her deal was. She turned her car on and ignored me then drove off. I tried to recall if the young girl could have been one of Valerie's students, just in case I had to explain myself.

I called Mike back, and he picked up immediately. "What the hell is this? You call me and then no answer when I call back?" he shouted.

"Relax! And where are you? I have to ask you something. It's personal," I said.

Mike didn't hesitate to give me the address to the house he was at. I drove to some sad piano music that Valerie had given to me. A collection of music she suggested that I was going to like. While I headed to Mike's location, I dwelled on that whole scene outside of the school. Something was off and felt as if there was a missing piece to this puzzle that had just puzzled my mind. And I knew that I would eventually find what was missing and complete this picture. But was I going to be happy with what it was about to be revealed to me?

I took a sharp turn into the driveway of the house. I could hear the saws cutting wood in the backyard, and to follow the noise meant to find Mike behind the operations of the saw. As I hit the corner of the back of the house, the smell of fresh wood swept the air and rolled off my face.

"Hey, man!" he yelled over the noise. He turned the machine off and took his face mask down to his chin. "Glad you made it. What's up?" Mike asked.

"Remember the two girls from the coffee shop? Do you communicate with Lisa at all?" I questioned anxiously.

At this his face wrinkled while he looked at me sideways. "Just a few times after the time that I had slept with her," he answered. Then he leaned his head away. "Why? Don't tell me you want her now?" he questioned.

I yanked his mask from his chin, letting it go quickly, just so it could smack against his jaw. "I'll take that as a joke!" I said to him, as I didn't want to get upset at him with his sarcasms and all. "I saw Anna today at Valerie's school. She looked as if she wanted to kick a field goal with my head," I described, then continued, "so if there's something that happened that you're not telling me, bro, I need to know," I demanded of him to answer.

He took his gloves off, stood in front of me, and crossed his arms. "I don't know what to tell you, Sebastian. I can't think of a reason why she would be mad at you. She should have been mad at me! For hitting on her friend when I was supposed to stay busy with her," he explained.

"The demeanor she carried was one of revenge," I described. He scratched the top of his head before remembering one detail he left out. "I don't think they even talk anymore," he informed me.

"How come?" I questioned.

"Well, after we had sex she didn't talk to me for a few days." Mike kept rubbing his jaw, trying to recall. "But…she did call to say she was sorry for crying in front of me. But then I asked about her friend. She called her a bitch and how she wants nothing to do with her," he explained.

I then shook my finger at Mike aggressively. "That's it!" I real-ized. "They had a fallout with each other," I added.

Mike looked like a cartoon character with question marks cir-cling around his head. "I don't see what that has to do with you," he said.

I tried to help Mike understand this. "When women suddenly hate each other, they end up hating everything about each other," I mentioned.

"Like I said, bro, if they were mad at anyone then it makes more sense for it to be me," assured Mike.

I began to grow worried about one fact. Anna knew a student at the school, and who knew if she knows Valerie. If Anna was mad at me for some odd reason I was not aware of, she would say anything to Valerie to get her upset with me too. I couldn't interrupt Valerie while she was working; I would have to wait and see if anyone had spoken to her. Or maybe nothing was said, and this was just my fear of losing her, playing games with my feelings.

I tried to keep my mind occupied working with Mike. After a while I just let it go and proceeded with Mike to finish the deck of a house we were cutting wood for. To add more thought in helping me forget what happened earlier with my encounter with Anna. I con-fessed to Mike what I was planning to announce to Valerie. While he was twisting his wrist and stretching out his fingers, relieving the tension buildup.

"Hey, Mike, listen," I interrupted. "I'm planning to get engaged to Valerie," I confessed, as we both sat down for a moment and took a break.

"That's good!" he shouted, and continued, "I knew you were going to take it there."

"No, you didn't," I blurted, as I backhanded the side of his knee while we sat side to side on the steps of the deck.

"I did!" he claimed. "When you started with Isabel you had this settled look of peace in your posture, and even in your walk. You seemed so sure," he described.

I sat with my ear toward him and was attentive to his descrip-tion of me.

"And now, bro, I see that same settling in you that I haven't seen in years." He laughed in relief and stuck his hand out to shake my hand out of respect. "That's good, man. You're on the right path," he said.

I looked down at my watch. It was close to 3:00 p.m., and Valerie would soon be done with work. "I gotta go, Mike!" I anx-iously blurted.

"What the? Okay, sure," he replied.

On my way to the school, another thing sparked my worry all over again. Valerie would usually call or text me before she got out. Even if it was to say something simple, and especially if she thought or knew I was coming by. I sped up a bit while this worry kept grow-ing. I pulled into the parking lot, and I took notice that her car was missing. This meant she must have left early then. I called, but this time when she picked up, her voice was duller than an old and abused butter knife.

"Yes," she answered.

"Baby, how come you left early?"

"Because I have a lot on my mind," she replied.

I knew right then that she must have just made a discovery to have her feeling this way. I immediately invited myself to see her at her house, but she refused.

"Sebastian, we need to talk," she suggested. The phrase that every man fears when a woman says it to him.

She then chose a location to meet her at. "Remember the diner we had breakfast at? You know, with your slick list of questions." Upset, she continued, "You can meet me there."

I exhaled slowly, fearing that my life with her was about to go backward. I drove down to the diner, with my body slumped in my seat, feeling lost even before possibly losing her. And looking like a zombie behind the wheel. Not knowing completely what to expect, I pulled into the diner and I saw her outside of her car. She was leaning against the driver door with her face to her feet, keys hung off her finger, with arms crossed. Not such a happy sight to see her in. I pulled close to her and parked. As I got out my truck, she had the dark-shaded raccoon eyes dead on my face. Her face was flatter than a board as I approached. I had just opened my arms to reach for a hug. But she put an open hand in front of me to stop me right where I stood.

"I didn't know that married women were your thing? I have to find this out elsewhere, huh?" she hinted, while her voice was slowly cracking.

"Valerie, I didn't sleep with no married woman! I don't know what story you were told," I assured her, then continued, "but that chick ended up with Mike, not me!"

"So…you two share women also? Hmm!" she assumed. I scrunched my whole face like a ball of paper going into the trash, in reaction to this claim. "What? No, no! That's not what I meant!" I yelled. I then lowered my voice a bit once I realized that we were in public, and I didn't want to draw any attention. "Valerie, yes. Mike and I met these two girls that we approached. And I know where you received this wrong info because I saw one of them at your sch—" I tried to explain, before she completely cut me off.

"Yeah, I know! Her name is Anna!" she shouted, with an evil shape to her lips as the name came out of her mouth.

I felt electrified and alert, as my mind was building its defensive statements to better defend myself. Only to be shot down by yet another discovery.

"I also found out about your ex…Isabel," she added.

My eyes went wide, and my jaw hung as my face became too weak to hold it up. I could see how she found out about Lisa, who I didn't even sleep with. But from what sources did she get her infor-mation about Isabel? And why? "How do you know about Isabel? I know it wasn't Anna who told you!" I questioned, as I demanded her to answer.

"You'll be surprised, us women know everything. We can find out about anything," she vented, with a look sharp enough to cut glass. And fire raging in her pupils.

"Look… Isabel was almost four years ago since we broke up," I explained, while I gave her the side of my face.

"Look at me, Sebastian!" she shouted, while I stood frozen in front of her sharp stare that was beaming right through me.

The hurt in her eyes was close to the hurt I saw in Isabel's eyes when I crushed her feelings for me; maybe this was why I looked away at first.

"What happened?" she calmly asked.

I straightened my face a bit and took a deep breath. "I cheat-ed… I…I took her for granted," I confessed.

"And you plan on doing the same to me?" she asked, in slow motion as her voice started cracking again. "My mother was a mar-ried woman when that scumbag walked into her life. And that bitch! Decided to leave my dad for him!" she yelled in agony.

Her eyes at this point became broken water pipes, as I saw a stream of tears that rushed down her face and down to her neck. She started to stab her finger in my direction. "I believed every word you said to me, Sebastian." Her mouth shivered violently when she spoke. "Every bit of it. You made me love you. You tricked me, you played with me!" she cried.

"I didn't cheat on you!" I shouted.

"Oh I don't know that for sure. But you lied to me."

"About what?"

"You told me you've never cheated, you told me you thought that marriage was something you would never disrupt," she recalled me saying.

I stopped her in her claims as I tried to save this moment of breakup. "I would never wreck a family, I swear. And how was I to confess to my destructive behavior? Huh? About someone I am not with anymore?" I asked.

She then again stood against her car, but now in silence, as I continued to try to save us. "I've done a few foul things before, and I knew you weren't quite ready to hear any of it just yet," I confessed.

"So lie to me, right? That's the best solution you can come up with, right?" she yelled while she smacked the sides of her hips.

"I'm sorry…" I whispered. We both looked around as a crowd, coming from the diner, started to develop. From all the shouting, we had done at this point.

She lowered her voice then leaned in close to my face. "I am not going to become like my mother," she whispered. "I refuse to be put through the hell she put us through, because of being in love with a pig."

"Valerie, you need to let go of this whole thing about your mother," I suggested.

"Thank you for fooling me," she cried.

My head was heavy with shame. My breath felt short and warm as if my ribs had shrunk, and my lungs ran out of space. Having a shortness of breath, I just listened at this point.

"You might fix homes and have all the machines you need. But the home I had for you in my heart, Sebastian. It's over. And there's no tool or machine that can fix what you've done to me." She opened her car door, sat down, and slammed it in front of me. Her window started to go down. I frowned and waited to hear what might be her last words.

"Oh, and your little bit of stuff you have at my house. You can pick it up in the morning," she added, then drove off and left me a dust of debris right where I stood. I felt embarrassed to notice that the crowd still stood there staring.

The next day I picked up clothes, watches, and tools that I had left in the basement. The tools that I had used to touch up a few things, and just never took them back. She didn't want for me to leave behind anything that may remind her of me. The brief time that I was there, if she wasn't giving me her back, she would pretend to fix her hair, just to block the sight of me with her forearm. I made a few attempts to speak, but she would breathe like a dragon with her eyes shut, or simply turn her face away.

With not a word to say, how quick can everything just change? That's how fast her feelings for me played like a magician and disappeared. One day she was in the grips of my arms; the next day that same space was nothing but empty air with a cold breeze breathing through my limbs.

Later that day I was in the back of the house chopping up logs, after

I had explained to Mike what had happened with me and Valerie. It helped relieve my stress momentarily. I swung the ax so hard, chunks of wood slammed against the garage door. I grunted violently, breathing heavily during the chopping. Anyone listening and not seeing would imagine I was in a brutal fight. I stopped when I felt my shoulder almost come out of my socket. "God! Damn it!" I yelped, as I grabbed my arm and sat on a chair.

Mike rushed out of the house. "What's your problem?" he asked, annoyed.

Just let me be." I sighed.

He shook his head not knowing what else to tell me. "Give it some time, bro…give it some time," he suggested, while he gazed over at the pile of cut wood.

I didn't even turn my head when I responded. "You know what I ask myself after everything that happens to me?"

"What's that?"

"If I've already learned my lesson. How much longer do I have to pay, for who I no longer am anymore?" I asked, with my forehead cramping from the stressful thinking.

He kicked a chunk of wood from in front of his foot. "All I can tell you, bro, is to chase her, man…or move on. Either way this world is going keep turning without you." He sighed in a helpless tone.

I could barely understand Mike, being that I was in another world emotionally. "I feel like I lit the fire, and now I'm burning in my own hell," I added.

Mike scratched his head then turned away. "I'm going back in the house, man," he mumbled with exhaustion.

To lie to a woman is bad enough. But I can understand how my lie had triggered a past that she had not let go of yet. The wounds of her mother's betrayal have cut through so deep to her. That they may take a long time to close or even worse, never. And from what I can see those wounds are dripping fresh blood still.

How can I fix both all at once? Is it possible? Or should I believe her when she told me I would never be able to fix this? I just figured when I met her that, since my past was already painted, and we had all the control over our present life, I could paint our future with a different brush and a brand-new canvas. But losing her this way made me feel like I just ran out of paint. She saw me under the same light she saw her mother's horrible ex-boyfriend. But not wanting to quit just yet, I suddenly started to feel determined to change that. Like a soldier drafted for war, I had no other choice but to fight, if I really didn't want to lose her. I would have to prepare my heart in the battle for her love.

CHAPTER 13

Feeling the Loss of Valerie's Love

A thousand truthful words, equals zero to the ears that you have already lied to.

A pile of my missed calls with a few ignored voice mails were left in Valerie's phone to sit and rot slowly. I could run a thousand words a minute, and each one of them could be heard clearly. But it wouldn't matter to the ears of the woman I lied to. Presents are nothing more than empty objects fishing for apologies. Postcards are just papers that belong in the trash. Her proving to me that there is nothing left for me to do exposed to me that if my actions meant nothing, my words meant even less. And all I was left with, all I had at this time, was my words. She has the choice now, to believe me or not believe me. But all I could provide to her choice was my honest words.

I did not want to take up the image of a psycho or anything around those lines. But this is what happens to a person when they're missing their love. We go through withdraws itching to be loved again, a love flu with heart conditions that is only healed by reviving what was lost. If it died, it died…but we don't want to hear that, or know that. We shake and breathe air into a body of love that has no heartbeat anymore, pale and stiff. But this body of love is deceased, and how hard it is to accept. Not only do we lose a part of ourselves, we almost forget who we are in the process. And this "we" that I'm talking about…is me at this point.

Sitting at home, I asked myself. What solutions are left to take? When the woman you love can't stand the sight of you and refuses to hear you out? Drowning in a sea of questions, where I couldn't even swim up to one answer. I get the worst interruption in such a lost state, a phone call from Old Man Rich. I was a broken statue just watching the phone ring. Was he calling to express feelings of anger and disappointment? Or was he looking for more work to be done at his store? I was pretty sure that his store by now didn't need much improvement if any. Before I could even get myself together, the phone stopped ringing, and he left a voice mail. Simply saying to come by the store when I get a chance.

Prepared for anything right now, I rushed to the store with my windows down and my radio off. Not only was I hurting over his daughter, I also had much respect for Rich. So if he shamed me, I would just hear him out and take the insult. What will it matter when I'm already half numb with all that has transpired? As soon as I parked, I slowly looked up at the roof. And I started feeling raindrops on my body and hearing the moans of Valerie that stuck in my head after that day we had sex on the roof. But emptiness started to settle in me, as I got out the car, entering back to reality.

I started to walk toward the store. A customer passed me by as I was inside. I then saw Old Man Rich at the register cashing out another customer. I stood still as he spotted me. I couldn't tell what was on his mind as he smiled at the customer but when he saw me his lips turned to a straight line. And his head nodded smoothly, appreciating my attendance. Quickly I moved out of his way as he happily walked the customer out the door then locked it. "How are you feeling, Sebastian?" he asked calmly.

The question just echoed inside my mind as I rubbed my hand on the back of my neck. Slowly I dragged my palm up the back of my head. "I don't know, Rich, I don't know," I answered, confused.

He chuckled, then invited me to his office. He reached for a clean cup. "Want a coffee?" he offered.

"No. Thank you, sir."

He observed my breathing as his eyes settled on my shirt. "Seems like you're out of shape there, and I'm not talking about physically," he added.

Before he could say anything, I immediately got up close to him and started to explain myself. "Hey, Rich, I'm sorry about Valerie. I know how things look, and I never cheated on her. I love your daughter, Rich, and I don't know what to do anymore." I agonized, while I slammed my body into a chair with my eyes staring into space.

"I didn't like the idea of you dating her in the first place, Sebastian," he confirmed to me, with his back turned. "But I did see a side of you that I felt was honest," he added.

"I very much was," I whispered to myself.

"She told me and showed me how you romanced her, but more importantly how you treated her. What I saw was the effort you were putting in wanting to be with my daughter." He sighed.

"I did. I put a lot of effort into our relationship," I declared.

He looked at me sharply in the eyes, with no intentions of blinking soon. "I also found out about you paying dinner for me and my daughter. Was that just to get in her heart? What really was the purpose of all your affection, Sebastian?" he asked.

I understood that he was her dad, and dads could be so protective over their daughter's feelings. But my jaw clenched, and my body spread wide for a split second, as I had tried to hide how upset I was over the question. "Rich, before I tell you that I'm not here to play games with your daughter, let me just tell you one small part of the reason why." I stood up quickly. "Not only have I done some wrong things the whole time I was with an ex, I also had the potential to do so much more. I was a boy at heart with a woman in hand, not knowing how to treat a woman." He seemed to be very attentive to me, which made me want to continue with confidence. "That's a mistake I'm not doing with another woman. And you're asking me what was all my affection with Valerie for? Because, Rich, failing to do so in the past cost me a good woman. And Valerie is just that and more to me." I sighed, as this felt like I had released some weight off my lungs. Even my shoulders were more relaxed.

He still had this serious mask of a face waiting for more "You said that's just one reason. What's the other?" Rich asked.

"That I know my true self can live in a happy home with who Valerie is as a person," I answered.

He started to show a slow, growing smile. "I knew you had feelings for her. You remind me of myself when I met Valerie's mother," he recalled.

I started to rub my chin, pondering, as I looked up at the pic-ture of Valerie on his wall where she was not smiling. "I'm sorry, Rich, I know that's a hard topic for Valerie to speak on," I disclosed.

"The separation of her mother and I had built our bond faster and stronger," he detailed after taking a quick sip of his coffee. "Although it was hard to move on, it all made sense once I met my wife a few years later," he said, as his face was glowing.

I was silent, giving him space to finish discussing, as he shook his head unhappily about the situation. "Valerie still holds on to what her mother put me through. But I don't want her to hate her mother," he finished explaining.

"That's tough," I simply replied.

He pointed at the sketch that she drew of him years ago, which hung above his computer. "She would draw and recite poems as a kid. Observing how talented she was with the arts, I helped and encouraged her. That's my daughter! of course," he declared.

I was just about to state my opinion on how great she was as a poetry teacher, but as soon as I opened my mouth he signaled me with his finger to pause. It seemed like what was coming next was important for me to pay attention to. "It wasn't until a while later, when I spoke to one of her school counselors. That drawing and poetry was a way for her to cope, with the hate she had for her mother," he explained.

I stood up from my seat with an offer to Old Man Rich. "If there's any way I can help, I'd be so willing," I promised him, with a hand on his shoulder.

"You can't… I know how my daughter is," he firmly assured me. After he pulled away, he then turned around. "Look, Sebastian, I won't tell her we spoke," he said. Then he continued, "It takes a lot even for me to change her mind. She's always been very sure of her decisions," he assured me.

I took one more look over at the sad photo of her on his wall. "Hey, Rich. Can I have that picture of Valerie as a gift?" I asked.

He gazed at me with a strange wonder in his face "Sure. Valerie actually hates that picture," he informed me.

"Oh! trust me, I know," I replied in reaction.

Before I could leave, he tapped me on the arm to leave me with a piece of wisdom. "I have to tell you…that both male and female, when younger, we both look for perfection in the one we are dating. In any and every molecule of that person. But as we grow as people, all we try to do is stay with the one who suits us best to our imperfect self," he said.

I shook his hand and thanked him for the good talk and the picture, of course.

Aside from looking gorgeous in the picture, I almost wished I were inside that picture. Or more like that moment when she needed much comfort and support. I was not a painter, but I stared at the picture enough times to paint it in the back of my mind. And mem-orized every curve of her posture and the tone of her demeanor.

A few days had gone by, and I was still not feeling like myself. After Mike and I had put up a fence in the front yard, Mike decided to stay with the customer. The family had invited us for a home-cooked meal, but since I felt I was falling apart, I just wanted to get home and get myself together. As I was on my way to the house, the truck was empty on gas. I turned into the nearest gas station in a side of town that I hadn't been in a long while. I felt at ease by simply standing there as I pumped gas. I had my head up, breathing some fresh air, with my eyes closed. Now that I was away from people, I felt deeply relieved and relaxed.

Suddenly a brand-new pearl-white BMW pulled in fast and smoothly on the opposite pump. I saw the driver as she walked off in a hurry, a lady who appeared to look familiar even though I can only see her backside. She entered the gas station to pay for her pump. She wore a two-piece black business suit, with this wavy brown hair that I knew from somewhere. As she had turned around leaving the station, my body felt it ran itself into brick a wall, when I realized that this was Isabel walking toward her car. Her whole walk was one to carry a team behind her. She appeared in charge of herself more than I've ever seen before. The determination in her demeanor was that of a leader and boss. It had been nearly four years since I last saw her.

"It can't be…it can't be…" I repeated under my breath to myself. As she came closer to her car, she started to squint her eyes at me. I turned away slowly, but I heard her steps leading toward me in slow motion as well. Where was I to hide my face of shame.

"Sebastian?" she asked with curiosity.

I spun around to see her look of surprise. She looked healthy and emotionally happy, with a glow to her whole aura.

"Huh? Hi!" she stuttered.

"Hey! Isabel, it's been a while," I greeted.

She smiled, and she shook her head up and down. "It has been, yes. It looks like you're still working?" she assumed.

"I'm just coming from doing some work, as a matter a fact," I confirmed. I glanced over at her car where I could see what appeared to be a baby seat in the back.

"Nice car," I mentioned.

"Oh thank you, we just bought it. I run my own business now," she added. She looked down to her feet emotionally. "And how's life other than work?" she asked.

I felt pressure all around my chest area, as the feeling of losing her combined with losing Valerie turned into a big python that had squeezed everything out of me. Not only did I not want to answer the question, how could I explain my situation to a woman, who has the experience to assume the worst of me? To confess to Isabel that I was at my lowest when she was at her highest. I become the loser frowning up at the winner.

"I'm doing okay. Everything is good," I muttered.

If anyone knew me best, it would be her, and I can tell that she knew something was wrong. Because she smirked with her head low and looked away. A look that I've seen before. "That's good, I'm glad," she added.

As she held her hands together, I noticed her keys dangling from them. Apart from her wedding ring, on her key chain there was a picture with three smiles on it. Hers, her husband's, and her daughter's smiles. She took notice of my face of shame while I had glanced at the picture. In reaction she spun her key chain on to her palm, and made a fist. My skull was a turtle shell as my face just wanted to hide away inside of it.

Whether it mattered at all, I couldn't hold it inside anymore, what I've been wanting to tell her for years. "Isabel, I'm sorry. I'm sorry for how I treated you," I confessed.

She tilted her head and smiled with a sparkle in her eyes. "Sebastian, it's fine, I don't hate you." She held her eyes closed for one second. "It just wasn't meant to be, that's all." She sighed.

Whether she said that because it was the polite thing to say, or she actually meant to say it, it felt good in my ears as this was some-thing I needed to hear, in order to bring a bit of peace to me. I was done pumping gas by now, ready to say goodbye, and I raised my arms for a peaceful hug, only to notice she took one step back and stuck her hand out at me for a handshake instead. "It was nice to see you too," she responded in a low tone.

When I thought I couldn't feel any worse, I ran into a part of my guilty past. What an awful state to go home to and be secluded. The only time to become scared of being alone with your thoughts is when they are based on guilt.

As I drove home. I had no choice but to connect what I saw, with what Isabel and I had spoken about when we lived together. She would try to tell me about patenting inventions, works, her wishing she had a clothing line, or how an LLC works. Wanting to go back to school for her master's before we ended, she also agreed to grant us one of our wishes, to give me a child. I see she had accomplished many of her goals, except that the child she had was by someone else. What was once late-night pillow talk with me is now a creation in her life made a reality. A reality that I had pushed myself away from being a part of.

CHAPTER 14

Letting Go

To pretend she never existed isn't the problem. There don't exist a solution to convince my heart that she was never real.

As the homeowner of my heart, how do I evict all the memories of Valerie that made its living inside of it? She showed me she loved me before she ever told me she loved me. My lips confirmed her kisses were pure, my arms felt the honest passion of her hugs, my eyes were the witness to her smiles of joy, the "I love you" phrase was spoken from a tone that was orgasm to my ears, and I could still smell the skin of her heated neck when her flesh would burn from my touch. To let this go so easily made zero sense to my five senses. But the sum of it all in truth is that she's not here with me anymore. And I'm left to do what I don't want to, and that's to accept the subtraction of her. Through this process my heart felt that letting go of someone meant losing. But my mind had to teach my heart that letting go of someone really meant making the space to win with the right one this time.

It had been a month and two weeks, and I had felt a small part of myself a lot calmer. I was occupied with more work and kept busy most of the time. Having such a long day remodeling with Mike, we had split apart and gone our own ways, as he was raking his feet on the ground, exhausted, and headed home to rest himself. I was end-ing my last job putting the door trim to the bedroom of a customer. Forgetting that I was on my sixteenth hour of work, I wasn't even aware of how exhausted I really was. I had worked my body tired this whole week, but for today I had done the most.

And there I was putting in the last trim of wood. I started to close my eyes every few seconds. The customer was a divorced lady Mike had randomly met recently, but left me alone to do the small work. And I had only decided to take up the job tonight only because it was a simple task.

"Are you okay?" asked the concerned lady from down the hall of the house.

"Yes!" I yelled back as I tried to open my eyes wide.

She stood from a distance, and I could see the white of her eyes as they shone in the dim hallway. More than likely she noticed me tired and dozing off.

"You sure you don't want any coffee?" she asked.

The fresh smell of new coffee was already sneaking into my nose from all the way in the kitchen.

"No, I'm fine…" I answered.

As she started to walk closer, I noticed she was biting her lips until she caught me observing the gesture. Even though I was offi-cially single, I wasn't looking forward to a sexual encounter, especially with a customer. I naturally ignored the signs of things heading that way. When she was up to the doorway, she leaned on the opposite side that I was working on, looking down at me, and started to spill out her curiosity. "You're a lot different from your friend Mike, not as social I would say," she mentioned, while she caressed her ankle with her other foot.

I looked down at her feet and said nothing but exhaled slowly. She was an attractive woman in her forties, with strawberry-red hair, matching the red of her soft-looking lips. Her pink sweatpants made the perfect pajamas, along with a white T-shirt that hung loosely on her upper half.

She was comfy as could be in her own home, and she was increas-ing her comfort level with me. "I can tell you're an overthinker. You should relax your brain every now and then, mister, um…what was your n—"

"Sebastian…my name is Sebastian," I interrupted.

"Sorry, I forgot already," she joked.

"The-wood-out-the-nail-this-trim-was…" I mumbled this gib-berish and immediately felt the embarrassment. That she took notice I was just stumbled over my words.

"Uh, you? What?" she blurted, followed by a burst of laughter.

"I'm so sorry. I think I need to sit for just a moment," I confessed to her as I wiped my face, shook my head, and tried to get myself together.

"Come here. We can sit on the sofa and take a break," she offered.

I was done with the job, but a few minutes to relax can be useful.

"I guess I'll get you that coffee now," she assured me.

I took notice of how decorative her living room was. It showed that she was alone and had time to be more creative around the house. Homemade diamond cups on the table, areca palm plants in every corner, with a perfect matching of an Egyptian theme to the room including her picture frames as well.

"Cream and sugar?" I heard her ask as she interrupted my wandering eyes in her living room.

"Sure," I yelped.

Along with her steps, I also heard her giggles as she entered the room. What must she be thinking? I asked myself.

She pressed her sight on my eyes as soon as I turned my head. "Your girlfriend must be wondering what time you will be home today," she hinted.

I gave her an distrusting look with a sarcastic smirk at the end. This was just another way of asking if I was taken or not. I decided not to even answer. She sat down next to me and handed me my cup. I wasn't sure if my refusal to answer had offended her. As we both had our faces to our lap, we both took a sip of coffee together, and kept embarrassingly quiet for a moment. I didn't want this to go from social to uncomfortable, so I tapped my finger on her knee to get her focused back on me.

"So how long have you owned this house?"

This was our second house together," she quickly answered. "My ex-husband and I were only here together for three years, but I've lived here for five," she detailed.

She rubbed her forearm lightly with a growing frown on her face. I just noticed that at some point she must have sprayed perfume on herself, as I had gotten a small scent of it tickling under my nose.

"Hey, I'm sorry, I don't mean to bring you back to a place in mind that bothers you," I comforted her.

"No, no worries. I'm fine!" she laughed.

You can say we were both in the same place in our road of life. Both alone and completely available. But I was the one growing curi-ous about her past marriage.

"Must have been a few years together," I mentioned as I dug for answers.

"Fifteen years. Yes, a long time," she recalled.

I took another sip of my coffee, which didn't seem to work since I was still exhausted. My curiosity had pushed me to know more. "Was it because of another woman?" I asked.

"No?" she answered, surprised. "If he did cheat, then…I never actually caught him," she added. She froze in her chain of thought, attempting to detail some more. "It was all about him. We lived in two different worlds, and I had to stop turning my world, so I could go and help spin his around," she described, distressed.

I tried my best to watch what I would say, as I didn't want any of it to be taken as if I was hitting on her. "I'm sure things will get better for you eventually." I sighed in a friendly manner.

She gave me a look as if she wanted to laugh, then put her cup down to cross her arms calmly. "There's no such thing as fantasies, Sebastian," she mentioned with a cold face.

I turned my head slowly toward her, wondering why the hell she would say that. "What do you mean by that?" I asked.

She started going into detail with examples from the point of view of a woman. "As a little girl you think your first kiss will be with some clean, smart, handsome little boy. But it ends up being with some scrub from school on a dirty staircase, skipping class. You then dream of losing your virginity to a charming boy who's romantic, wealthy, in a place filled with flowers. It ends up being in the back of an old car with cigarette burns everywhere, to an asshole who is screwing other girls anyways. After that you promise yourself that you'll have a child with that one guy you'll live your whole life with, and get married and die. But he turns out to be the worst deadbeat father you'll ever regret you ever met," she expressed, with her eyes staring into space.

"Wow," I responded. This sounded horrific to me.

"You see, Sebastian, there is no such thing as fantasies," she fin-ished saying.

"So what do you do then?" I asked.

"Well, you try to be happy with whatever you're left with. Don't kill yourself over what might never be," she answered, unemotional.

What I took from this example was that nobody is perfect and neither is their journey, but I kept my opinion to myself in case she somehow took offense to it.

"I have no girlfriend, to answer your question from earlier," I said. "I just…sorry it's just too much to get into detail," I explained, apologizing.

She started talking about her job as a nurse, just to change the subject. We were having a good talk together, and I was pleased to share words with this woman. But my sleep was creeping from my feet, under my flesh, up my muscles, and weakening up to my brain as my eyes started to twitch. I shut my eyes for a second, and went into a deep sleep filled with hugs and soft touches. I felt a light snore breathing calmly from my lungs. I was so tired I didn't even notice how fast I fell asleep.

I woke up three hours later in the darkness of her living room, wrapped in a blanket. Forgetting where I even was, I jumped and screamed for a second as I sat up, with my forehead sweaty. I looked around the living room. The hallway lights come on and then the living room lights next, as the lady walked in.

"Hey, did you have a nightmare?" she asked.

Coming back to my senses, I started to calm down my heavy breathing, apologizing for the outburst. She laughed and sat next to me. She appeared so satisfied to look at my face, as she put an arm around my back and one hand on my knee. I started to rub and squeeze my face as if I wanted to take it off. "I need my own bed," I declared.

She couldn't stop smiling. She sighed and confessed. "You made me feel good tonight," she mentioned.

I was confused as to why and how I made her feel good. Did I just miss something? I wondered. I looked around, and I even touched my pants. Which I was still wearing. I turned to her, lost.

"Uh…we didn't have sex, did we?" I asked.

"No we didn't," she simply replied.

"But we did cuddle for a few after you fell asleep. You don't remember kissing?" she asked.

I started to remember her leaning in to hug me as I was dozing off, but it was a blur, along with a soft touch on my lips before falling asleep. "Wait…you kissed me!" I pointed out.

"Yes, but you kissed me back while we were cuddled," she claimed. She leaned in and lowered her voice. "You don't remember anything else, right?" she added calmly.

"No, I don't," I promised her.

She moved the sheet away from me and fixed herself in her seat. "We cuddled and you were in such a deep sleep. But then from out of nowhere it was almost as if you suddenly woke up, hugged me, and asked me." She paused her smile, which had stretched wide. "You asked if I knew how much you loved me. And then you kept saying how you'll never let me go," she gushed.

It brought me back to the memory of Valerie, and how I would cuddle her and express my love for her minutes before we would fall asleep. It was obvious that I was sleep-talking, and this behavior, although unconscious, had all to do with the fact that I hadn't been with nobody since Valerie. And the fact that it had only been almost two months since I lay in bed with Valerie.

"I know you weren't talking to me, but it felt so real what you said. It was so good to hear it, and I felt so secure when you hugged me," she expressed.

My chest started to hurt; my throat shrunk just a little. As I didn't want to remember how much I cared for Valerie, because of how I was proceeding in my life trying to forget these feelings, I was learning to forget the taste of Valerie's mouth on my tongue, the smell of her skin on my body, which has already faded away. I was even forgetting what the sound of her voice was like. I've must have suppressed my emotions into my subconscious if they were spilling out in my sleep.

I jumped out of my seat and aggressively fixed my clothes. "I have to go! I have to get home now," I told her, anxious. As I rushed to grab my tool bag, I sped my way out of her house.

She probably thought I was crazy or that something was wrong with me. At this point, what she felt about my behavior meant nothing to me. I had no intentions of seeking her comfort in the first place.

Working my ass off and letting Valerie go seemed to work at first, but emotions are never worn out by anything we do in order not to feel them. There's no doctor anywhere with a remedy, or a therapist with instructions on how to forget someone you've loved. The heart has its own deadline of holding someone there, and the expiration date is only known for itself and not known by its owner. Even our own common sense can't convince our own hearts to forget so easily.

Again, I was bombarded with decisions. I tried getting her back after she left me. Should I try one my time? Or should I give myself space and some more time to forget her? Was it all supposed to be so difficult? But I had to realize too, if love was so easy maybe our soul wouldn't learn and appreciate the true value of it once we get to capture it...

CHAPTER 15

Valerie's Father Has Some Strange News

Don't underestimate the fear of being loved; that kind of fear is the car-bon monoxide to our breathing. We're not even aware that it can kill us inside slowly.

From the pegboards, storage cabinets, storage racks, rolling tool draw-ers, charging station to organize the power tools, and a few machines to add to the countless equipment that we'd use, I loved our garage and how we've come to put everything together. And it was that time to not only clean and dust, but also organize the mess we had been too busy to keep up with recently.

Mike and I had been arguing about sports until we had gotten exhausted about the subject. He then asked about the other night when I was at the divorced lady's house. Since he took notice that I had gotten home late from a job that was supposed to be quick, I detailed everything that happened, and him being his usual self. He had his own distinct way of viewing the whole situation.

"And you just left?" Mike asked in an attacking manner.

"Yes, I did, that simple…" I answered carelessly.

He took a seat with a power drill in his hand, pulled the trigger, and growled to himself under the spinning noise of the drill.

"Mike, I don't give a damn about what you think!" I shouted.

He took his finger off the trigger and started to tap his forehead with the drill, before putting it down and standing up. "Sebastian. That woman is divorced, and you're single," he said.

I stood quiet and took the drill from aside of him just to put it back into the charging station where it belonged.

"Even if I was tired, I would've been all over that!" he admitted.

"Oh trust me, we know," I assured him.

Maybe I would've enjoyed tasting her body that night too. But she messed my whole mood up with her description of me sleep-talking. I left that part out when I told Mike what happened. I was too embarrassed to admit about the sleep-talking I did.

It suddenly came to mind a lesson I meant to run across Mike, which I had learned a long time ago. "Mike, I want to teach you about this thing I call 'why did I ever?' or why did I never?' example I put together long time ago," I advised.

"Come on, man. What the hell is that about?" he whined, annoyed.

"Sit your ass down and listen," I demanded.

He took a seat, and here I started. "You go about your normal day, nothing different. Except you run into this gorgeous female as you walk into a convenience store, and she's coming out. She smiles at you and looks you up and down, licking her lips. You are so caught off guard that you freeze and do nothing. By the looks she gave you, you're thinking you could have gotten her number. And maybe even took her home that night, we don't know!" I said.

He burst out in laughter, shaking his head yes, relating to the scenario. But before he could interrupt me, I stopped him so I could finish. "I know exactly what you're thinking right now. "Why did I never say anything to her? We could have been hanging out doing all sorts of things in bed by now. Right?" I asked.

He nodded. "Now here's another way it can happen. You and her exchange numbers, have sex, fall into a relationship on accident, maybe even have a kid! She turns out to be very toxic and evil, you never saw this coming to you. Now she ends up being the worst ex-girlfriend you wish you never met…what do you say then?" I asked.

He crossed his arms, and at the same time we both say, "Why did I ever say anything to her? I wish I never talked to her that day."

I chuckled a little. "You see, Mike, you never know what you are actually saving yourself from. It could be good, it could be bad," I explained.

He appeared to be pondering, and then under his breath, I heard him say, "Why did I never? Or why did I ever? Hmm…"

I go back to finish up some organizing on the storage cabinets. "Sebastian, you can be odd sometimes," he joked. "But I still got love for your crazy ass," he added.

I ignored him and kept inspecting around the garage. Mike's phone rang, and I heard him pick up and talk. "Yeah, he's here…he probably left his phone somewhere," he said.

I waved my hand at him, wondering who it could be. He didn't say a word; he just handed me the phone. It was Old Man Rich sounding so serious, I was assuming he was upset. I asked if every-thing was all right.

"They could be better. But hey listen, kid. Are you home?" asked Rich.

"Um yes, I am," I answered, concerned.

"Hey, Rich, I'm all ears. If there's some kind of issue, man…" I added.

I heard him exhale slowly. "Let's just say I have some strange news for you, buddy, you can take it how you feel." And he hung up.

The dullness in his voice was thick. He spoke as if he were hold-ing up a heavy box and couldn't wait to put it down. I told Mike about the quick conversation and the impression I received from it.

And like usual, he took it seriously for a bit but then went back to his humor. "Well, we can kick his ass. It is two of us," he suggested, laughing.

My eyes went narrow, and my face was so still as I stood face-to-face with Mike. He patted me on one shoulder and excused himself. "Sorry, bro…I mean, let's see what it is. It might not be anything," he assumed.

A few minutes had gone by, and as we finished up in the garage and I swept up the last bit of dust at this point, Rich pulled into the driveway, suspiciously slow. Mike and I looked at each other strangely for a split second. Then I just quickly walked out of the garage and straight to Rich's car, which was a navy blue Audi with dark windows. Before I could even get to the driver door it swung open, and Valerie's foot touched the ground. I stopped right where I was standing and pulled my head back to scan her whole body from her feet to her face. I was surprised to see her arrival at my place. She smiled, but I was the one who frowned. I turned my face away from her and sat right in the steps of my porch.

"I told my father to trick you so that I could surprise you," she confessed excitedly.

"I don't like surprises," I reminded her. "And he sounded so serious when we spoke," I added.

"He's a good actor, right?" she joked.

"Valerie, what do you want?" I burst out in frustration. "Did you meet some guy and it went bad? And now you run back to me?" I yelled while I was squeezing my hands together in a fist.

She sighed and shook her head. "Uh? No?" she said, with a look of sarcasm. Then she sat down slowly right next to me.

"I had a long talk with my father," she mentioned.

"Hmm…he must have said some good stuff to convince you to visit me today," I added.

She gave me a quick rub on my arm in which I leaned away slightly. "No, Sebastian, he didn't try to talk me into anything. I make my own decisions," proudly she claimed, and then continued, "when it comes to guy advice I trust my father all the way. He tries to explain to me the inner workings of a man the best way he can." Then she turned to look at my face as I had my head down. "He thinks you're very sincere," she said to me.

I know she could sense the numbness in my demeanor. And to not have her discouraged, I simply told her, "I'm listening."

"Well he made me do my research, and I found out that Lisa and Ana are not friends anymore, but enemies," she disclosed. "Lisa was probably trying to make both of you look bad for whatever rea-son," she added.

I was still upset in which I had an outburst. "Are you serious, Valerie? Over some dumb female talk of some dumb bitch I never did anything with!" I shouted.

"Sebastian, you still lied to me about not cheating on your ex. You didn't have to do that!" she argued.

There was no point in me trying to defend myself. So I sat there with ears open and waited for whatever was coming next.

"But when my father told me that men can make the most fool-ish mistakes even if they love you…I…" Her eyes soaked up as her voice was slowly cracking. "I started thinking of all the good times we had, more good than bad. Whenever I was with you, you made me feel good," she confessed.

Only in the absence of my presence did she recognize these feelings I brought out of her, I thought to myself. "I wasn't just trying to get in your bed. I wanted to be at peace with you, not just have a piece of you. Everything I ever did for you, everything I ever said, came from what I truly had felt for you, Valerie," I promised her.

"Had? Well, from the feelings you had…do you still think you have any feelings for me left in you?" she asked, with her voice get-ting weaker by the second.

"I don't know…just let me be for a few minutes," I asked of her. She was okay with giving me my space, but before leaving she questioned, "Hey, why do you like that picture so much? The one you asked my father for?"

I smirked at her and shut my eyes for a moment. I then started to head to the truck to grab the picture because I kept it there. I grabbed it and then stepped in front of her and handed it back. "Because I see beauty even in your sad moments. I'm not sure actu-ally, I just think it's gorgeous," I said. "Nothing personal, but you can have it back," I added.

She held it low by her belly as her face wrinkled at the sight of it. I said good night to her and walked into the house.

Why does someone only return to you once you had let them go, or are in the process of letting them go? When feelings are dead or dying for this person, is it healthy to attempt to give it life again? We learn from the past and move on, but we should never stay stuck in it. But is it ever a part of our future to return to our past for one more fixing? Do I give my back to her? Or do I just get back with her? This was my anger spinning my brain into a tornado of question marks.

I was getting nauseous by the second, as I sat in my living room to a silence that was screaming pain inside my body and vibrating my flesh and bones. I looked around at this cold room, and for a second almost forgot I even lived here. I couldn't let my anger take over my decisions. I did miss Valerie; it just hurt to get walked out on by the one you cared about. And If my mother were here, she would tell me, "That is how Isabel must have felt when you left her for no reason."

Chapter 16

Every Story Has Its Own Way of Ending

You make me forget everyone I ever started with, when I remember that it all ends with having you.

Only one week had gone by, and Mike and myself had landed a big project. A brand-new house with lots of work to be done. There were other guys scheduled to work around us. The plumbing and elec-trical job had been done already; the insulation had been finished a day ago. For the meantime we had drywall and interior textures to work on followed by the exterior finishes. But for the near future we had other jobs ahead of us in this new house once we got past these things first.

We hadn't left yet as we were loading the truck with useful stuff, and here was Mike arguing with me in the meantime.

"Sebastian, she came back for you!" he reminded me. "You should be, right now, cooking her breakfast in the morning or any of that romantic crap you do!" he shouted, being sarcastic while he fixed his heavy-duty belt.

"Yeah, but why all of a sudden? What happened? Did it go bad with someone else so quick?" I argued.

"Who cares, bro!" he said, while he smacked lint off his shirt and pants. "All another man is, is a list of things that you are not. So even if she did go on a date with someone else, she left her heart back here with you," he expressed.

I looked at Mike up and down then started to mock him. "Whoa! I see I've had an influence on you man, my protégé." I laughed while I clapped my hands.

"Man, shut up…besides, she told you she hasn't been seeing anyone. She looks honest," he claimed.

I was actually not upset anymore; I just didn't know the right words to say if I was to reach out this time. "You're right, Mike," I confessed.

I then laid my back against the bed of the truck, as I took in what Mike had just said. In a daze I heard the echo of Valerie's sweet laugh rushing through and out my ears. I looked at the ground and imagined her seductive walk, with her delicious legs, tapping her cute feet moving in my direction. But most of all, the touch of her lips and the heat coming from her hugs that tingled my flesh and weak-ened my insides.

What was I still doing there when I should be in her arms?

"Mike, I gotta go," I blurted.

His arms spread wide faster than an eagle taking off. "What? But I don't mean now!" he pleaded.

"Too late, bro, I'll talk to you later. You guys don't need me," I assured him. He wasn't happy, but he drove me to take action for my lady. I'll blame him for that later.

I jumped in my other truck that I would use every now and then. I drove off and called Valerie. I wasn't sure where she might be, but I was to soon find out. She picked up, excited, "Sebastian!"

"HI, baby," I gushed. But inside I wanted to scream *I love you.*

"I painted a canvas for you," she quickly interrupted. I wondered why she threw this at me so fast. "I know you don't like surprises, so I figured I'd tell you before I hand it to you."

"Oh…well, what is it?" I asked.

"Sorry, that part is still a surprise," she said as she laughed in relief to be speaking with me.

I shook my head even though I did laugh under my breath. The important part was that we were speaking in peace with each other.

"Some things just don't change, huh?" I added.

"If you're not busy, can you meet me at the park where we took that walk? Remember? When you were recovering from your leg?" she asked.

I happily agreed and proceeded to go meet her. Soon as I parked next to her, she had her window down waiting for me. She gazed into my eyes and smiled. At this moment, with just one look of her eyes, she spoke to me for hours in just a split second. Everything felt much better, even the air felt new and fresh. I rushed out the truck taking fast steps toward her. Her seductive walk out her car had not changed a step. I received one of the tightest hugs and delicious kisses that I had missed very much.

"You're looking good and healthy as usual," she mentioned. "I look okay," I replied as I brushed off the compliment in an attempt to remain humble.

I ate her alive with my stare as I gazed at her up and down. "And as for you! Sweetheart, mmm…more gorgeous than a royal queen from back in Romania, Portugal, or…one of those," I described.

"So you're going to go there, huh, back to kings and knights?" she asked.

"I'm not trying to. But I would love to be your king at night," I gushed, then licked my lips.

She sighed with a face that buzzed with joy. "Now that you are here with me, I remember what it feels like to be happy again," she murmured. "Oh! Let me give you the canvas."

As she reached toward the rear door of her car, my eyes were already wandering with curiosity over her shoulders. It was a painting of her face. The face from the picture that I gave back to her, but just that. "What happened to the rest of your body, sweetie?" I wondered.

"You're asking for too much, my love," she joked, laughing. "I thought I was showing sadness, but my frown was not enough to mask the beauty you somehow had the X-ray to see. So I figured I'd make the painting of just my face instead," she explained to me.

It was still a gorgeous work of art that could fit like the miss-ing puzzle to my bedroom wall and bring life to the room. I sat the canvas in the passenger side of my truck, and we then took off for a stroll in the park. Side by side with the pace of two married couples, walking down the aisle. We conversed.

"Why did you decide to grow so distant from me even though it was only two months?" she asked.

"Because, Valerie, whether with me or without me, this world will continue to turn. I can sit and hurt, or I can keep it moving even if it hurts my feet to step away," I detailed.

She listened while she nodded. "Your father even told me how sure you are about your decisions," I added.

As we walked in the same rhythm, it felt similar to the first day I was here with a cane, recovering. But now that my leg was fine, I was still here recovering, with the same companion. Only this time it were my feelings that were healing up.

"You know, Sebastian, what you told me about letting go of the drama with my mother…you were right," she confessed.

I grabbed her hand and brought it to my face, just to rub the back of her hand softly all over my lips before kissing it. "It's okay, my love, even I have things I have to live with," I comforted.

"Sadly there's…there's just some scars that make us who we are," she added.

"Look. I have a past, and so do you. I have my own problems and responsibilities, and so do you, Valerie. Bet when we both are together, just you and I, I don't think the world around us should even exist. Not even our past should be a welcomed guest in our quality time," I suggested.

She looked at her belly and smiled. "That's enough with past problems. What do you see as far as for your future, Sebastian?" she asked.

"Well, since Halloween is only a few months away… I was wondering if you can be my pumpkin?" I flirted.

She rolled her eyes while she chuckled for a second. I then reconsidered what I said, and how I felt about what was up ahead of us. "All I hope for is that you remain in my future. However, it goes with us, there might be times when the motion of our journey won't be pleasant. During ups and downs, either way it moves. I want to move with you," I comforted.

She slowed her steps for a moment, getting emotional "Good… because I'll need you there, Sebastian," she mumbled, with her voice cracking. "Where there's a will, there's a way," she added.

"And no matter the will, Valerie, I'll never be away," I replied. She stopped suddenly and grabbed her head, appearing as if dizzy out of nowhere.

"Are you okay, my love?" concerned I asked.

"Sorry, I felt nauseous for a moment. My mind's been running. Maybe it's that…and I've been busy as well," she explained.

"Hey, I know it's early but, maybe in a few hours we can go wherever you want and have a drink?" I offered.

"No, no. I don't drink anymore."

"A glass of wine won't do anything to you. It doesn't have to be something heavy," I persuaded, trying to convince her for a good time out later on.

"I would love that, but no, let's do something different," she suggested.

We had gotten near a park bench where she wanted to sit and rest her sexy feet.

"Last time I was here, I was the one with the cane struggling to keep up with you. And now that we haven't walked as much as before, you want to take a break already!" I teased.

"Of course, honey! You're the gym rat in this relationship," she replied.

By this time, I felt as if I have learned a lot, especially recently. But one thing that bothered me was what I was told by the lady whose couch I fell asleep in. I decided to share these words with Valerie, and express my own opinion of this knowledge the lady tried passing on to me. "Not so long ago this divorced lady explained to me how 'there is no such thing as fantasies,' according to her," I said.

Valerie gave me an evil stare, as if I had an affair that I didn't inform her about. I had to make it clear to her that it was just an encounter and conversation before I continued. "Although the lady had a point because of her experiences, what I took from it, Valerie, was that 'there is no such thing as perfect people with perfect circum-stances,' but I didn't want to lead us into an argument," I explained.

"I can see her point in a way," Valerie related.

I went as far as giving a further example from one of my child-hood memories. "When I was a kid, we had a mechanic in the family who made me a two-foot statue of what looked close to a Transformer toy. A man of steel made from screws, nuts, and other metal parts. I brought it to school, and not only did the other kids want it, one teacher almost bought it from me. But it was a gift given to me, which was priceless," I said.

"And what's the connection between this and what the lady told you?" Valerie asked.

"The connection or what I understood from it is that you can always take what appears to be scraps in your life and turn it into something special. Just because some fantasies have died doesn't mean we have to stop dreaming and creating," I expressed to her.

She looked so comfy sitting next to me. Slowly and softly she would blink her eyes, while massaging her sight all over my face. I leaned back and took a silent moment once she tapped on my wrist with her fingers. To signal to me of some knowledge of her own to share. "What you just told me, Sebastian, reminded me of something I've learned and applied myself," she said with all smiles.

"What's that?" I asked.

"Do you remember when we first had breakfast and I stressed to you how you're not really my type?"

"Yes, I'll never forget you said that to me," I confessed.

"Well, I've always believed that once in a while it's good to go out of our type, out of what we lust, or are so routinely used to. You never know where your love might be hiding." She sighed.

I couldn't help but notice that she kept playing with her purse. Was she nervous about something that she didn't know how to tell me? Or did she simply wanted to leave from this bench where we sat in? I kept growing curious but didn't dare ask, but I finally I felt I had to know.

"My love, are you okay?" She stood silent. I then continued to dig. "Is there something you want to tell me that I need to know?"

"Yes, actually there is," she confessed.

I didn't know what to expect, therefore I started getting nervous myself. She took a deep breath and squinted her eyes. "I hate the fact that you don't like surprises," she said aggressively.

I didn't grasp what was her big deal with that part of me, but I tried to understand and maybe even work on changing this trait that I've always had. "I don't know, sweetheart, but if it bothers you that much I'll work on that," I promised her.

"Good. I think you should," she suggested. "Speaking of which, I do have one more surprise for you," she said as she glanced at me sideways.

I cringed to the sound of that word surprise, but I decided to put my ego aside and listen to my sweetheart.

She took her purse off her lap, then placed it on my lap. "In this purse I have a big postcard. Open the purse and pull it out," instructed Valerie.

I slowly opened it and reached. Pulled out an all-white post-card with no lettering on it anywhere. I then looked at her face with curiosity as to what may be inside. "Hmm…no words, I see," I sar-castically added.

"And what's inside needs no words either, my love, open it," she demanded.

Once I opened it, I saw the printing of an ultrasound. The development of a baby. "Wha…what? Um…" I stuttered, and almost lost my whole breath just to realize what this meant.

She couldn't help but laugh and cry at my reaction. "How much does it surprise you that you're going to be a father?" emotionally, she asked.

"I…wow, give, give me a second," I stuttered. I tried to get myself together as my brain sunk this all in, slower than quicksand but all at once.

"I'm three months pregnant," she informed me, with her face blushing and a tear of joy hanging from her eyelash.

I touched her small belly, and not a single hair on my body was sitting flat. It was like we had a lip-stretching competition, since we both couldn't stop smiling at each other. Could this be the real reason she reached out for me and wanted me back in her life? Whether this assumption was true, or just a negative thought that was running through my mind at this moment, it didn't matter to me either way. Because what I didn't get to finish with Isabel, I would now finishing with Valerie.

Her love for me was buried, but it rose out of the grave, like a rose out of the grave. More beautiful and loving than ever. I truly felt I deserved this, and this time around I had no plans on messing up what could be a wonderful future together. "Does your father know?" I asked.

"Hey, silly, when are you going to learn that he knows every-thing? I tell my dad everything," she reminded me. "He was the one who told me that you were going to react the way you just did once I told you," she recalled, laughing.

"I mean…it's not like you're informing me about the weather

tomorrow," I joked.

She giggled then added some sarcasm to my statement. "You're too funny. But hey! I can find out about the weather tomorrow if you'd like me to," she said as she maneuvered her neck in a mocking fashion.

"You don't need to, but whether it's foggy or cloudy tomorrow, my decision of having you in my life is as clear as day," I flirted.

We then kissed for a few minutes, pressing our bodies against each other. Strangers would walk by, chuckling under their breath, but who cares? I'd display my love for this woman any and every-where I could.

"So since I gave you back that picture of you, can I keep this one of the baby?" I asked as I placed it against my chest.

"Of course! Why not?" she answered.

Just to stare at the picture, I could already see the scissors in my hands. I would feel like I was cutting my own vocal cords right off after cutting the umbilical cord. Because this gift of my new child will leave me speechless. I can see my child going to school, playing at day care, and everything else. I might have been lost in the moment get-ting ahead of myself, but I couldn't help it. I was so happy I couldn't control hiding it at all. And even though this ultrasound is black and white, it still brought color to my eyes. And as for Valerie, she just helped me paint the colors in my life that would make my dying journey come alive again. My companion and I, and the gift of a precious new life we both brought into this world together.

Through ups and downs women can be so strong naturally. They have the stomach to take in the pain of providing by them-selves, they can stomach starving themselves to feed their seed, plus they can stomach working insane hours. And also toward us men, they can stomach our wrath and teach us how to deal with emotions. They can stomach taking care of us when needed, they even stomach our defects and insults, which is nothing that a man should be proud of. When you look at it, this is no wonder women give birth. Because that same strong stomach is what's able to hold our beautiful child for nine months. Another special reason to admire our companion that walks this earth with us men.

The End

About the Author

William Sanchez is a thirty-nine-year-old Puerto Rican born in Connecticut but raised in Massachusetts. He's always been into writing since he was about twelve, writing lyrics. By the time he was a teen, William was very much into poetry reading and writing poetry as well. As he got older, he slowed it down a lot and even stopped at one point. Right out of high school he worked labor jobs for years. William's current job is as an armed guard delivering money. He fell in love with poetry again and decided to pursue his sudden dream of being an author.